The GRAVE MARKER

Story, cover illustration, and design by

Don LaCroix

Order this book online at www.trafford.com
or email orders@trafford.com

Most Trafford titles are also available at major online book retailers.

Note for Librarians: A cataloguing record for this book is available from Library
and Archives Canada at www.collectionscanada.ca/amicus/index-e.html

Printed in Victoria, BC, Canada.

ISBN: 978-1-4269-1331-0

*Our mission is to efficiently provide the world's finest, most comprehensive
book publishing service, enabling every author to experience success.
To find out how to publish your book, your way, and have it available
worldwide, visit us online at www.trafford.com*

Trafford rev. 6/29/2009

 www.trafford.com

North America & international
toll-free: 1 888 232 4444 (USA & Canada)
phone: 250 383 6864 ♦ fax: 812 355 4082

For Fran, and her loving support

Preface

M Y REASONS FOR writing this story are several, not the least of which is the seldom told history of the East African ivory trade that was centered in nineteenth century Tanganyika and Zanzibar, and its economic relationship with the Connecticut towns of Deep River and Ivoryton.

Perhaps, a more important motivational influence was my desire to illustrate the humanity of the slave, for which I chose the fiction genre, which allowed the opportunity to develop the main characters, not as passive victims of their unfortunate circumstance, but as complete and authentic persons with natural skills, lively souls, and the free will to respond uniquely to the abominable condition of slavery.

The final incentive for writing the Grave Marker was purely for the joy of creating a compelling story. Though told through history, sometimes touching upon real people and events, I chose to add the adventure of fascinating places; the impractical absurdity of a slave interacting with Victorian royalty, the interior heart of an artist, the fierce loyalty of a protector, the interaction of slaves from two different worlds of enslavement, the timeless intrigue of an ivory serpent cane, and the serious moral questions involved with the ivory trade, as raised by students in a modern classroom who decide to alter history, only to find themselves an essential part of the story.

An apology is due the reader, perhaps, in the sense that I have made no attempt to accurately portray the real personalities of the historic people involved; the Cheneys, George Read, Sam Colt, Queen Victoria, and the various Omani Sultans. Though reasonably woven into the plot, I confess to merely creating entirely from imagination their fictional personalities and behaviors, which I molded, as needed, to fit my tale.

Acknowledgments

*I*T IS BECAUSE *of the enthusiasm of April Winterson and her class, with their heartwarming response to my initial writing, as well as their encouragement, that I continued on, eventually coming to the stage of publishing this story. To them, I am deeply appreciative.*

I'm also grateful that my friends, Tom and Art, were willing to properly steer me as I ventured into this task.

A special thanks to Mary Pollack, for all her work editing the manuscript, and her wise suggestions for its improvement.

CHAPTER ONE
A mystery solved, or is it?

FATHER NOVAK COULD see the man through the splattering rain and condensation on the rectory window. It was the rawest of days, just above freezing, windy and raining heavily; the kind of miserable New England day on which no one voluntarily goes outside, no one except this tall black man with an old rumpled suit, dark glasses and white cane. Was he blind as well as completely unaware that he was getting drenched?

If he was blind it would be a surprise because he certainly seemed to be paying a lot of attention to one old grave marker right next to the side entrance of St. Joseph's Church; the passing years and careless footsteps had victoriously rendered the originally engraved name impossible to read. Hadn't this very isolated grave been the subject of a record search just last spring by the Parish Improvement Committee, including some fairly competent folks who were unable to find a trace of who it was that was buried there? Moving that grave would allow for expansion of the side entrance and what the parish needed more than anything was an elevator for the older folks to attend Mass. That grave was holding up the project, and Father Novak suspected that this strange man might have the solution to his problem. He reached for his umbrella, already shivering, from the thought of having to go outside in that wretched weather.

"The Lord gives me challenges every day," he muttered, smiling to the benefit of no one but himself. Undaunted, he opened the rectory door and was immediately confronted by the tall stranger who was standing inches away in the pouring rain without benefit of a hat. He apparently was just about to knock on the door with his cane; it was white, intricately carved ivory, looking in all its artistic splendor, like twin twisted serpents.

"May I come in please?" said the man with just a hint of a French accent.

"By all means, please do. I'm Pastor Novak."

"I know," said the stranger in a matter-of-fact way, and not bothering with the nicety of introducing himself; he brushed by the priest casually sharing with him much of the moisture off of his drenched suit.

"Would you like some hot coffee?" the priest reflexively offered.

"Cognac would be fine, if you have any, thank you," the stranger said. Moving his cane, he searched for a place to sit.

"Sit over here by the fireplace and warm up," the priest said, wondering whether to take him by the arm. It wasn't necessary because the stranger seemed to move readily to one of the upholstered chairs by the fire. It was Father Novak's favorite chair, and it was about to be treated to the soaking of its life.

"I'll see if I can find some cognac," said the priest pondering what he was about to learn from this stranger, who obviously had a mission of his own to accomplish.

"*However does he know who I am?*" worried the Pastor. "*I certainly would remember meeting him before; after all, I haven't met that many tall black blind men. Have I?*"

"Will rum do sir?" asked the priest as he ruffled through the kitchen cabinet, "I have a bit left from Father Alfred's last cooking adventure. I'm afraid it's rather old though."

"That will be just fine, Father Novak," came the deep-voiced reply above the crackling fireplace.

It took a moment for the priest to find his lone silver tray and a glass sufficiently suitable for presenting rum to his uninvited guest. Pouring himself a cup of well rested coffee, he settled down next to the strange man, and waited for him to begin the conversation. He didn't, leaving the priest with that horrid feeling of having to make nice empty conversation, about nothing, until his guest was ready to divulge his real purpose for appearing here at St. Joseph's, obviously unsuitably dressed, for such miserable weather.

"I do have to apologize," the priest began, tugging uncomfortably at his Roman collar, "but I don't recall ever meeting you before, Mr….. "

"You haven't," was the stranger's almost casual reply. The man was still not willing to identify himself.

He then appeared to look directly at the priest; he was rigorously cleaning those dark glasses that were completely fogged up from condensation caused by the warm fire.

"I've never been to Connecticut before," he said, sipping his rum in a rather courtly fashion, betraying, perhaps, someone with an aristocratic past, someone well trained in upper class manners. "To be truthful, I've never even been here to America before yesterday. I just came up from your New York City this morning," he said, causing even more curiosity for the priest.

"I noticed that you were … *I can't say looking, can I?*" Father Novak thought to himself. "I noticed you over by the church earlier," he finally said, dropping his caution, and revealing what was on his mind, "standing by our old grave marker."

"Yes," was his all too short reply.

"You seemed to be quite interested in it," the priest pressed on, hoping for more information.

"Yes, I am."

"May I ask why? It might help solve a real mystery for us."

"You wish to move the grave," replied the stranger.

"How is it you're aware of that?" asked the now bewildered priest.

"Your committee was researching the occupant's identity."

"Yes, we were, earlier this spring. Do you happen to know who is buried there? The headstone is well worn and…."

"I'm afraid that you'll never find anyone who can give you the answer to that particular question Father Novak."

"May I ask how, you sir, or anyone else, can say such a thing with such certainty?"

"It is because, Father, there is no one buried in that grave; there never was!"

The priest, mouth agape, put down his coffee cup without looking and spilt the remainder of its contents all over the small table, and on Mrs. Cornish's hand-crocheted doily.

"Then, what is buried there?" he asked incredulously, ignoring the spilled coffee for the moment.

"It's a long story, father," said the man fingering his ivory cane casually. "Do you have any more rum, please?" he asked, then, settling back in Father Novak's favorite chair, he announced, "I shall tell it to you."

CHAPTER TWO
An aristocrat arrives

M R. MACREADY WAS at it again; he was causing the class to become deeply involved in learning about history. This time it was about what he called, "Post Civil War Slavery." The classroom atmosphere was already charged with excitement, when the discussion stopped abruptly as everyone's gaze turned toward the just opened classroom door. Standing there next to Headmaster Rheingold, was a tall, young black man with a smile and a large back pack in his hand decorated with the familiar "B" that anyone near Boston knew stood for their beloved Red Sox.

"Excuse me class, I'd just like to introduce you to our newest student, Jason LeBlanc. Jason and his sister, Michelle just arrived here from France. Michelle is in Mrs. Holbein's room."

"Well, we are happy to have you here, Jason, and we have an extra seat over there at Samantha and Jonah's table. For your sake, I hope you like to read because that's all they talk about over there," said Macready.

"Oh, but I do Sir."

"You may call me Macready, Jason, Mr. Macready. What part

of France are you from?"

"Paris. Is there any other?" he replied with a grin.

With a touch of borrowed pride, Headmaster Rheingold interjected, "Jason's father was an ambassador for France for many years and is presently working in Paris researching unusual medieval literature."

"Well Jason, welcome to our class, we were just about to get the homework assignment, from which you will get to escape, but only because you missed most of our lead up discussion."

Macready was not doing Jason any favor. This young man thrived on doing homework, or any other kind of learning for that matter. It took but a couple minutes for Macready and the class to realize that.

"Okay class, we're just about ready to enter the research phase on the abuse of slaves, which strangely took place after the Emancipation."

"Got a hint for us Mr. Macready?" asked Sarah.

"I do, Sarah. It didn't happen in the South. It happened, you might argue, right here in the North, in abolitionist New England."

"Mr. Macready?" It was Jason.

"Yes, Jason?"

"Did it have anything to do with Monsieur Scott Joplin?"

Macready looked puzzled, he hesitated to respond, at first, not wanting to embarrass a new student by calling attention to his first error, but then he suddenly understood the wisdom of this young man's answer.

"This classroom has just been gifted," he thought.

"Why yes, I guess that it does, somewhat, Jason, though I'm amazed that anyone could figure that relationship out."

"Mr. Macready, is it all right if I try the homework?"

"Oui," Macready jested.

"Merci," replied the sophisticated immigrant, enjoying the

banter.

Jason was a distraction in the computer lab: as many students were gathered around him as we're busy researching."

"Imagine," said Sarah to George, "a real ambassador's kid in our class."

"He can't be too smart," said George with a slight grin.

"Why's that George?" Sarah asked, surprised at George's comment.

"He's not a Yankee fan--it's a sure sign of his being feeble minded."

George, as smart as he was, was the only Yankee fan in the school, and relished the notoriety such a position brought him daily, living here in Boston, the enemy's camp.

"What's with Jason's comment to Macready about Scott Joplin?" Sam asked Jonah.

"I don't know. I haven't the slightest idea, but Macready surely saw some connection."

"Let's try the internet. I'll bet it's easier than we think, if we start with Scott Joplin or ragtime music," said Sam, while pretending to move her fingers around an imaginary keyboard.

"So you're a Sox fan, Jason?" asked George, looking to re-establish his credentials as the school's only Yankee fan.

"Actually, I'm not."

"You're not a Sox Fan?"

"I'm not even a baseball fan," said Jason. "That book bag was my sister Michelle's idea. She insisted that they'll love me in Boston if I wear this fancy letter "B" on my book bag."

"Not us Yankee fans, but you're okay with me just because I finally found someone around here that is not a real Sox nut."

"No, I'm a reading nut; that's my sport."

That comment caught Samantha Quimbly's ear. "How much *do* you read Jason?" Samantha inquired.

"Oh, very much I would say."

"Have you read over a thousand books yet?" Sam continued

her pursuit.

Jason looked off into space doing some mental calculation. "Oh yes, quite a while ago," he guessed. "I've read more than that amount, if you include the Latin and a little Greek with the French."

Samantha inhaled deeply, and then came out with it. "If you like to take real reading adventures, Jonah and I have some reading friends who'd like to meet you Jason?" she suggested, with a slightly mischievous grin.

"Sounds good to me," he replied, anxious to get together with committed readers and also make new friends.

"Let's meet after school for a few minutes and talk about it okay? Right now, I've got to get going on Macready's research. Do you have any hints to share Jason?"

Jason just grinned, "Why don't you just look up Monsieur Joplin?"

It wasn't until the next morning that the Scott Joplin connection was finally made. It came as a complete surprise to most of Mr. Macready's class, though George and Jason already knew the answer, few others could put it together.

"It looks like a couple of you figured out that the answer was the Ivory trade out of Southeast Africa."

Those that hadn't yet understood what Macready was getting at were waving their hands from all over the room.

"I don't get it," said Jonah. "What does the ivory trade in Eastern Africa have to do with New England, Mr. Macready?"

Jason almost begged to answer; but Macready wanted to find out if anyone else actually figured it out. George, as usual, did.

"I found out that it was really Connecticut that was responsible for using most of the world's ivory," he correctly answered, "and much of the slave trade in East Africa was about getting the prime ivory to that market. Slaves were captured, often by conquering tribes and usually sold to the Arab traders. They would carry their precious ivory cargo from as far away as 1000 miles into the

African interior. When a slave would falter and die, they would just buy or capture more along the way, selling the last surviving ones in the Zanzibar slave market."

The class sat quietly pondering the horror of what they were hearing.

"But, why is Connecticut at fault because those people treated slaves badly?" asked Sarah, once again causing a deeper level of thinking with the simplest of questions.

Mr. Macready answered this one because it gave him a good opportunity to explain what was behind the ivory trade. "It had to do with things like ladies combs, buttons, billiard balls, walking stick handles and yes, especially ivory piano keys. Connecticut, Sarah, was where most of the world's ivory was brought for processing. Although it was illegal here in America to use slave labor after the Emancipation Proclamation was signed, the slavery that was used in the ivory trade was far enough away from America that few people here were aware of the human and animal destruction that occurred. The immense rum and spice industries also drove the slave trade; a fact that might surprise most of you students who think slavery was just about cotton and tobacco in the South."

"How does Scott Joplin tie into all this cruelty Mr. Macready? Wasn't he an African-American?" Jonah Crane asked.

This time Macready let Jason LeBlanc do the teaching. Jason smiled, pleased for the opportunity to show his knowledge. He began, "After your Civil War, right up through WWI, came the age of the piano. First the rich, the bourgeois had them, then the saloons, the dancehalls; just about every middle class home wanted to have a piano in their parlor. In addition to the traditional gospel songs, just around the turn of the century, Monsieur Joplin's ragtime piano music came alive and encouraged even more piano playing, which in turn caused more demand for ivory, though by then, the abolitionist movement had effectively reduced much of Zanzibar's slave trade."

"So then, the ivory keys on the piano are the Scott Joplin connection, but why was ivory processed in Connecticut, Mr. Macready?" It was Sarah again.

"Well it had a good river port, a seafaring history, and plenty of skilled craftsmen with Yankee ingenuity." He pointed out that just a couple of companies in two lower Connecticut River towns were responsible for the trade.

"Deep River, and Essex, particularly the Ivoryton section which became one of the earliest company planned communities in the USA, both grew out of the town of Saybrook, which was located at the mouth of the Connecticut River, where easy access to the open oceans of the world was available."

"Are we going to get your usual trivia connection to this unit Mr. Macready?" asked Sarah who seemed to know just when to ask that question.

"Well, I do have one great point of interest. When the Connecticut ivory business was starting to boom in the early1880's, there was a fire at the Deep River Pratt and Read plant, which burned down completely. The result was a loss of about 15 tons of prime ivory, destroyed forever, and utterly wasted, not to mention the cost of both the human and animal lives that it took to bring it there in the first place."

Jonah began twiddling the bronze key on his neck. "Fifteen tons of ivory. Did that really have to be wasted?"

"Jason raised an eyebrow, wondering what Jonah was getting at, but Samantha caught the meaning of his comment and panicked. *"Oh no--not Africa with the jungle full of snakes and biting things--he wouldn't dare!"*

But, she had known Jonah for too long already and she knew that he just might dare anything.

There was one extra bicycle chained to the iron gate at the old McClelland Library that Saturday morning. The abandoned silent buildings and sidewalks of old North Street seemed to not be impressed with the reality that an ambassador's son had chosen to pay them a visit.

Jason had begun to have second thoughts about agreeing to go along with Jonah and Samantha to join their reading club. Who wouldn't, after viewing the deteriorating condition of the old McClelland Library; its cracked windows, chipped masonry, worn stone steps and vacant isles, now but a hollow testimony to the fruits of centuries of great authors and scholars?

"This place is more like a book museum, rather than a library," Jason thought.

Sitting on the floor, surrounded by a pile of books, was the elderly Miss Margaret, reading an old manuscript. As people her age often do, she was speaking the words out loud; "Respice, adspice, prospice."

"Study the past, the present and the future," whispered Jason ever so softly.

A surprised Miss Margaret, having excellent hearing, turned to look at Jonah and Sam's new friend and asked, "And just where did you learn Latin, young man?"

"At the Sorbonne, in Paris Madame," he replied.

"But, you're too young…."

"The youngest ever, they said, but I was just there for the literature and the languages. I was fortunate to have a good private tutor for much of my education; except now, my father has decided to send me here to add a Boston view to my experience."

Miss Margaret, smiled softly, put down her book, and rose, adjusting herself to be presentable for this delightful young man.

"And why, are you visiting us here at McClelland's, such a long way from the Sorbonne, and Paris?"

"Jason's our newest class member Miss Margaret. His dad was an actual ambassador in France," said Jonah jiggling his bronze key conspicuously, "We thought that you and the professor would like to meet him."

Samantha, acting very much like Jason's personal advocate,

interjected, "He has read well, over a thousand books already, some in Greek and Latin."

Miss Margaret, with a newfound twinkle in her eyes, reached for the phone, dialed and began, "Professor Kincaid? There is someone here that I believe you are going to enjoy meeting. Yes, we'll wait for you, and oh, please bring that rubber stamp of yours with Priscilla McClelland's signature. I'm certain you'll need it."

It was a short while later that Jason was presented with the opportunity to join the Bronze Key Society. He had no trouble promising to keep his reading adventures secret, nor trouble in limiting his Gothart Collection reading to whatever all three kids agreed to, but he seemed hardly curious about having to learn the three words of the oath: *Gothart, Trahtog, and Gothart,* dismissing it as some sort of silly club ritual, not yet realizing that those words might make the difference between life and death. He had little idea yet of the real value of being able to access the Gothart Collection of books.

"I've may have heard of that book collection before," he said.

"You have?" wondered a surprised Professor Kincaid, "Do you remember where?" he asked, glancing nervously at Miss Margaret?"

"I think, from my father, Ambassador Leblanc. He's considered somewhat of an expert on unique medieval literature and I'm almost certain I've heard him mention the Gothart Collection before."

The four previous members of the Bronze Key Society looked at each other with some trepidation. Could it be that there was someone else alive who knew the secrets of the Gothart Collection?

"Jonah and Sam," Miss Margaret asked, "Will you get Jason his membership key please, and show him downstairs? Perhaps all of you would like to do your homework together down in the Gothart Room?"

Jonah couldn't hide his excitement about this reading adventure any longer and blurted out his intentions. "We have to save tons of ivory from being destroyed by a fire in Connecticut, Miss Margaret, would you and the professor care to join us?"

Glancing at the professor, she responded, "Perhaps we will Jonah. We haven't done anything quite so noble in a while, but first, don't you think you should show Jason the advantages of being a Bronze Key Society member and the Gothart collection?"

This kind of talk made Jason very nervous and he began to have even more misgivings as they descended the old library stairwell. His doubts increased when he was told about the secret lock in the first wooden door, and even more, when in the next room he encountered the large gate containing the lock that matched his new bronze key. It was a bit too intriguing. "*Why,*" he wondered, "*do we need to read down here in this dungeon-like atmosphere?*"

He changed his mind, abruptly; once Sam opened the final door to the Society's reading room. He stood in awe at the magnificent library in front of him, with its rows and rows of books and plush furniture; it was more like something that he would expect to find in an old European castle. He knew immediately that he had found his new home. He had no idea of the real reading adventures that were yet in front of him, just a few feet away in that room off to the side, with the sign above the door that read, *The Gothart Collection.*

"Okay," Jason said, as he headed into the Gothart room, eager to find out how good this book collection really was, "let's find out about that Connecticut fire."

"Wait!" Both Jonah and Samantha said in unison.

"Why?" Jason asked, surprised at their reaction.

"Well," said Sam, "we really do need to talk first, Jason."

The seriousness of their tone convinced Jason that they were telling the truth, but what they were saying was simply not believable.

"You don't really mean to tell me that we really can go back to the place and time that we read about in those books?"

"Yup, and sometimes you can even become someone else," said Sam, impishly.

"What if I said, I don't believe you?" he said with a nervous grin.

Jonah offered the solution saying, "There is an easy way to prove it, Jason."

Jason's smile slipped a bit, but he had gone too far in doubting them, now he would have to follow through.

Samantha turned to the Gothart Collection and started looking under Connecticut, 1880's, where she found what she wanted and she took it over to the table in the center of the room.

"Here it is. This picture is of Main Street in Deep River, CT in 1881, and was made just a few days before the big fire. Do you two gentlemen want to go for it?"

Jason was really getting nervous now. He was intrigued with the possibility of going back in time, but he was also wondering if he was dealing with really crazy people. His curiosity won the battle. "Let's do it," he said.

Jonah quipped, "At least at this time in history there was no war going on." Sam, who was relieved, only because Deep River wasn't the darkest part of the African rainforest," added, "Nor will I need my bug juice."

The three moved to the book and placed their hands together on top of the old picture. Jonah and Sam watched with amusement as Jason's face changed from a smile to a worried frown; the manuscript began to shake; the room began to be enveloped in the aroma of the sea-freshened, Connecticut air; time and space reached out to grasp them.

Upstairs, the sound of the book slamming shut reached the professor; he smiled and asked, "Where did Jonah say we were travelling to this time, Miss Margaret?"

"A short trip to Connecticut, to save some ivory," she replied, "back to the 1800's professor."

"Toll free, I assume," he said, taking her arm. "Shall we join them? Perhaps, I'll become a priest for the occasion," he smiled again and then asked, "And what will you be?"

"Oh, I'll decide when we get there, Professor. The important thing is to help save that ivory."

CHAPTER THREE

Tanganyika (modern day Tanzania) mid 1800s

IT WAS JUST a flicker, the slightest of movements, but it caught the eye of the young hunter Duma, who became as still as the bones of his ancestors, just as he was taught by the elders. *"Not even the beat of your heart should be seen nor heard,"* he repeated their words to himself as he concentrated on the area from which he detected the movement, allowing just his eyes to move slowly, examining each blade of grass and leaf in the bush. The gazelle, the first of a group of nearly a dozen, was unable to detect Duma's scent. Though the soft breeze was in the hunter's favor, it did detect something else over in the tall grass by the waterhole, it would not move yet. Thump went it's hoof, trying to get whatever was out there to expose itself in response, but the young hunter had been trained well, expecting such behavior; he remained unflinchingly still.

It was the animal's tail that flicked again, giving its position away and sent a signal to the hunter that it was about to relax its alertness soon. Duma's keen eyes detected still more movement. There were others in the herd. It would be harder to make a kill with so many cautious eyes watching. He would wait patiently until they started drinking, then they would be most vulnerable to the thrust of his spear.

Out of the corner of his eye he detected another movement to his rear; further down the lake shore; other animals were coming to drink, or was it another hunter from the village? "*As does the cunning leopard, keep your eyes and head on your quarry,*" he reminded himself, irritated that he could be so easily distracted.

He could smell the pungent musk from the gazelles now, as they began to move out of the bush to the murky water's edge, seeking the life-giving liquid. He had made this distance, a mere seven meters or so, when he practiced with his spear many times, back in the village, with the other young men. It would be an easy kill and there would be a feast tomorrow. Slowly, he raised his spear; he had spent many hours perfecting the sharpness of the jagged blade that it might cause great bleeding. The nearest animal had just lowered its head to drink when he thrust it forward toward the gazelle's chest. It struck right behind the shoulder, as the alarmed herd bolted like missiles, leaping over the tall grasses. It was a simple task to find his quarry. Following the bright wet blood on the trail wasn't necessary as he could hear it thrashing, ending its life without ceremony.

Duma, no longer the wary hunter, had his game down and began to hastily work the warm carcass, disemboweling the antelope to cool the meat quickly before it began to spoil in the hot African sun.

Engrossed in his task, Duma failed to notice the danger creeping up from behind him until he noticed the shadow that had moved across the bloodied sand, resting momentarily, just under his arm. It was the shadow of a spear and it was pointed at the back of his neck.

His reflexes and adrenalin took over immediately as he turned rapidly, swinging his arm at the spear, knocking it aside. Lunging at his would-be assailant with his skinning knife, he slashed him across his chest, forcing him to crumble. There were others, shouting and running toward him. Now it was he that was the hunted. He turned, desperately fleeing for his life, for he knew this tribe well; they were the dreaded hasimu, one of the tribes that captured slaves for sale to the Arab ivory traders, the *muuza*.

Few run as fast as those fleeing for their lives and few, if any, back in the village could match Duma in speed, for had they not named him Duma, which was the Swahili word for cheetah? In the village games he outpaced them all, but this was no game now; it was to be the run of his life, for his life.

Duma knew he had one advantage, even against so many. They would not use weapons to stop him, for a wounded or a dead slave has no economic value. They would have to capture him alive and healthy to get the most reward from the flesh traders.

His legs, now but a blur of movement, headed directly along the lake shore where there would be no obstructions to slow him down. He began to accelerate, quickly opening the distance between himself and his pursuers.

It was a serious mistake; the net caught him perfectly, and brought him down, rolling and thrashing, helplessly, as several men rushed to contain him. The struggle was surprisingly brief as the immobile Duma was instantly helpless. They too, knew how to hunt and he had made the fatal mistake of running right into their trap. Their quarry was down and now they would secure him for the trials he would face ahead.

He could hear the wailing voices even as they were binding his hands. It was his own village that they had raided, taking captive anyone of value, and killing the rest; the old, the weak and the young. The heavy smell of drifting smoke told the horrid story even before he heard them coming. They emerged from the bush, a groaning line of captive slaves, their bodies bent in defeat, in contrast with the happy chatter and lively steps of their victorious captors.

Even from the distance, Duma could see his brother Mlima, the tallest of all men in the village and his sister Jala, who he recognized by her familiar black and white striped garment. His heart sank when he realized that his mother and father were not visible, having been discarded in the burning village as too weak and burdensome for the long journey to the East African coast. His soul was ripped from his very heart, as he well understood the coming misery. They were now no longer humans, but mere objects who were afforded no more dignity than the village dogs; they were of far more value as possessions, to be traded on the blood and tear-stained streets of the Stone Town slave market in Zanzibar.

Duma was immediately given special attention by the chief porter who commanded that he be brought over to him. The ivory necklace he wore had singled him out. He made it from an old elephant tusk he had found neglected on the outskirts of the village.

Duma had received two special gifts in life: his ability to run, which had failed him already; and his ability to patiently carve beautiful designs into ivory which would alter his life. When he was only ten years of age, he made his mother an ornate bracelet carved with patterns of cheetah paw prints, which he carved somewhere in all of his work. It was the most attractive bracelet in the village, and soon Duma became known as the official village carver of ivory. Having the keenest of eyes and the surest of knives, he turned dull ivory, discarded by nature, into prized ornaments that brought delight and social status to their wearers, who readily displayed Duma's cheetah paw as proof of the high value of their ornament.

Duma didn't completely understand what all the fuss was about until this "Chifu," speaking Swahili, demanded to know where he got the necklace that he had just cut free from his neck. Even then, in the midst of a moment of deep sorrow and despair that he was experiencing, Duma felt a strong sense of pride in what he had made. Holding his head up high he answered that he was its creator, "Duma," he repeated, "Duma!" though he was unable to point to himself because his arms were held tightly by two large tribesmen. The chief porter smiled, displaying a mouth full of carved and discolored ivory teeth. He had found a prize slave. Duma thought, *"His mouth is like the grin of a hyena. I shall call him, a hyena, a 'fisi."*

The Chifu recognized that a slave with such talent would bring him more value in the slave market than some of the other slaves. He shouted instructions not to damage Duma unnecessarily, unless he tried to escape. With luck, the hundreds of miles of cruel struggles and disease that lay ahead on the ivory trail, would not kill him as it would so many others. As they began to swiftly move off, Duma was given a lead spot, right behind the ivory-toothed Chifu, who probably wanted to insure that his new prize remained valuable. Strangely, this caravan of human bondage was not bound in chains or placed in wooden yokes as Duma had heard would happen, if one was unlucky enough to become enslaved by the traders.

It was early the next day when they came upon the large opening. Captives, both men and women, were actively involved in moving ivory tusks into large piles near several grass huts while their captors prodded them with spears or threatened them with a blow to their flanks with clubs. They were quite careful not to damage any arms or legs; the slaves had to have the ability to carry out the heavy ivory. A few other Arab guards sat nearby watching the labor carefully, hoping, almost eagerly, that any escape attempt would give them an excuse to use their matchlocks.

Within hours, the caravan was readied for the march of death, the many hundreds of miles' journey through the African interior to the Indian Ocean coastal town of Bagamoya where the ivory, and those slaves still alive, would be stacked like objects onto dhows and transported the twenty-five miles or so to the most morbidly fascinating island in East Africa; Zanzibar, where both slave and the ivory they carried would then be put up for sale.

Duma and his brother Mlima were prodded to lift a large tusk to their shoulders. Like a heavy parasite, that tusk would be their constant companion over the many weeks ahead. They would become as one with the tusk.

It is a quirk of life that the strangest of games are those that hopeless captives play. As the days passed, Duma tried to shut out the wailing voices of the other slaves, first by concentrating on the massive plains and then on the forests and mountains, mesmerized by all the new sounds and visions he was discovering as they moved along the trail. Already he was further from his tiny village than he had ever been and strange terrain, the bushes, the trees and the animals, presented themselves as a special challenge to him, to be memorized forever, anything to avoid thinking about the scourge and humiliation that was to be his life now. Duma's keen eye for design and shape began to record in his memory the ingredients for a lifetime of raw material for his art work, should he somehow survive. His eyes became his paint brush and his carving tools as he moved along, ignoring, as best he could, the weight of the heavy ivory tusk pressing into his shoulder. He painted and carved in his mind all he saw. The strange fern-like plants with their fingers hanging straight down, as if they too had been imprisoned, didn't escape his notice. The occasional beasts that rushed away in haste, the soft feathered birds that protested as the caravan invaded their peaceful swamps, and the myriads of long-tailed monkeys that scattered and chastised these strange creatures below for interrupting their play, also became part of his long list of potential motifs. There were times, even entire days, when he was so engrossed in observing the beauty of the living African forests, the swamps and the mountains, that he almost forgot that he was but a slave, no longer his own, free to do what he wished.

Once, while having a rare rest stop along the trail, a silent communication took place. Duma made his cheetah paw print sign in the soft earth for Mlima to see. Mlima, for his turn, took the small stick and made an up-side-down "V" mark. It was the sign of the mountain-the mark of Mlima.

For Duma, there was yet another special moment when the two things, slavery and his art, came together. The caravan had stopped for the night and Duma lay exhausted, hungry, and in pain from carrying the heavy ivory all day. In minutes, most of the caravan was asleep, save for a couple of guards sitting by the fire, loosely clutching their guns, half watching, and half sleeping. The sounds of the forest were just coming alive with their weird symphony of night noises, when Duma noticed it slipping slowly through the branches of the great banyan tree just above his head. It wasn't a particularly large serpent, but it was magnificent in the way that it moved, wrapping its slender body effortlessly around each branch, embracing it momentarily with each scale on its white belly as it passed further into the night. Even in the dim firelight, its brilliant red eyes were visible.

"*Where is that creature going,*" he wondered. No longer burdened by the shouts or jabs of the porters, he realized something he had never felt before, even when he was creeping up on the wary gazelle. It wasn't so much that the snake could move in the most interesting fashion, or that, it too, was probably hungry and searching for some food. It was a more simple matter, but it was the most important matter of his young life.

"*It is free,*" he realized, "*to go wherever it wishes, whenever it wishes.*" It was then that he fully understood the beauty of that serpent. It had what had been so cruelly taken away from him, freedom. At that very moment, lying by the fire inhaling the strong musky smells of the decaying forest floor, he imagined himself, a serpent, crawling through the tangled branches of the darkened forest, going ever farther and farther away from the ivory and the guns; and he wept.

"What good are my fast legs now?" he silently whimpered. *"I shall be like that serpent someday; not running away fast like the cheetah would, but moving slowly, deliberately touching each branch as I move away, but only the ones that I choose to touch."*

Later that night Duma had a dream about serpents, how they were captured and put into an ivory cage by the slave traders, and how he, now a serpent, was able to slide under the matt on the floor of the cage and escape, never to return.

No one paid much attention to the small herd of cattle that had been grazing on the sparse grasslands several miles north of the slave caravan as it had passed by weeks earlier. No one noticed that particular tsetse fly land on a cow's bony rump and draw out the precious red liquid to feed the larva inside its body; for such little things are regularly lost in the constant stream of daily attacks by the deadly tsetse. Nor did anyone notice that the fly bit several in the slave caravan the next day; no one, except the victims that felt its death causing sting. Duma's sister Jala was but one of the slaves treated so poorly by nature. Slaves aren't protected by their caravan masters from nature's numerous pests that they are forced to withstand; the death causing tsetse, the aggressive bees, vipers under their feet, or one of several species of huge biting ants. Mercifully, the agonizingly slow and horrible death typically caused by the sleeping sickness, would not come to Jala. Death on the ivory route, this time, came quicker for her.

It was the smallest of events on the trail and hardly an interruption of the caravan. One of the guards who noticed Jala's head nodding while she was moving recognized instantly the most visible symptoms of sleeping sickness, the inability to stay awake in the daytime. Human property that was diseased was worthless. Property that was worthless was to be disposed of promptly, only to be replaced at the next village, or the one after that.

There were the usual shouts as a guard snatched away her

provisions and gave them to another slave, doubling his burden. Jala, in her black and white striped dress, stumbled off into the dense forest only to be greeted by a cloud of thick blue musket smoke and a lead ball in her back. Duma started to move toward her, but he was abruptly halted by the pressure of the muzzle of the Arab *Chifu's* musket in his back. The grotesque man promptly displayed his ivory teeth in a hyena-like grin. *"Fisi"* thought the helpless Duma, *"If I ever get free, I shall skin him like the fisi he is."*

It was several days before Duma was able to control, first his anger, then his depression, over his sister's cruel death. He had thought long and hard about the evil that had befallen them and decided that he would not become a victim. He would not succumb to the anger and despair of his situation, because then the slave masters would win. He made a vow then and there that would serve him the rest of his life. He would allow his body to be the property of whoever owned him, but not his spirit, and by so doing he would always remain free. He would not resist or allow himself to resent the lashes of the whip, nor the forced sweat of his labor. He would conquer his enemy by keeping free his spirit. If he was to be a slave; he would become the best slave there was, but it would be his free choice to do it. It was apparent that even his gait stepped up a bit faster in the days and weeks after that, and he once again was able to return to gathering visual images that made the terrible journey to the African coast seem like someone else's bad dream.

CHAPTER FOUR
Zanzibar

I F EVER THERE was an international crown jewel of commerce during the mid to late nineteenth century; it was Zanzibar, that 60 mile long, Indian Ocean island off the coast of Tanganyika, where East and West corroborated in the business of trade and wealth building. This was the island to which seafaring merchants traveled from all corners of the world, to purchase or trade in exotic spices, the most desired ivory in the world, and to mankind's shame, captive humans; the black slaves who carried the ivory out from the deepest disease-infested interior of southeast Africa. A captive in the interior would be forced to carry the heavy ivory tusks for hundreds of miles, work more properly done by beasts of burden, only to be enslaved in the spice trade, or sold in the Zanzibar market, if they were one of the survivors.

They were all involved; just about every nation of means, just about every religion, and every race, driven by the promise of riches produced at the cost of millions of innocent black lives. Few in the centuries' old business that took place all over the world, were blameless of the trading in human flesh. The Arab

25

traders, the Hindu financiers, the Christian ivory merchants, and even the African tribal chiefs who also made a profit selling their own race as slaves, were all part of the obnoxious slavery business.

Culpability might include, as well, those masses of people in faraway places; who never directly took part in the atrocity of slavery, never saw the abuse of their fellow humans, never heard the musket that brought a wretched runaway down, never felt the crack of the whip, the cutting chains, the wooden neck yokes, or the weight of the heavy ivory tusks, but demanded the goods that were produced on the backs and bodies of humanity's "less than human," humans. They all shared in the guilt, to various degrees.

Though many human victims contributed to the success of the ivory trade, if you would call it that, it is also unfortunate that the destruction of untold numbers of elephants and hippos unnecessarily occurred over a span of many decades, in order to obtain sufficient amounts of the precious white gold.

It was ivory that brought George Cheney and his bride, Sarah to Zanzibar to begin raising their family, many thousands of miles from the Connecticut River towns of Deep River and Essex where the precious ivory bought by merchants like Cheney appeared on river docks just as any other merchandise for processing, unencumbered by the realization that each tusk of white gold came to be there at the expense of many black lives.

It was that same demand for ivory from those same Connecticut towns that had also brought Duma to the slave market of Zanzibar, a horrible journey, hundreds of death-filled miles from his home near Lake Tanganyika.

That the life of a simple, artistically talented, black slave from the deep interior of Africa and a wealthy white ivory merchant from America would somehow intertwine here in this exotic place remains a mystery that would, nonetheless, alter events miles away and many years later.

Duma had never experienced anything like Zanzibar. The streets of Stone Town were lined with many large white square-shaped buildings that betrayed an Arabian influence and acted as a backdrop for the masses of busy people with strange skin colors and even stranger clothes, as they moved excitedly through its narrow streets. These odd houses were somewhat alike with their massive wooden doors decorated individually with iron or brass handles and hinges, many with pointed iron knobs jutting out, perhaps to keep the war elephants from battering them down. The narrow alleyways reminded Duma of the canyon walls of rock, etched out by the eroding rivers he had seen on his journey here. These canyon walls he marveled at, realizing instantly that they were man-made.

Being in Zanzibar made him as fascinated as he was fearful for his own well being.

The stories, told by the elders in his village, spoke of the evil places where slaves were sold, but they spoke of dark and frightening surroundings while this was excitingly bright and intriguing to Duma. It was not at all as he had imagined.

The manacles and chain Fisi had placed on his thinned wrists before they left the mainland cut deeper as Fisi hurried him along through the narrow streets with a jerk and a tug now and then. Fisi had long ago decided to keep Duma as his own slave to sell to some rich merchant for an extra price because of his ability to carve intricate designs in ivory. He carried in his robe the carved necklace that Duma had made, ready to display to any potential purchaser who might appear wealthy enough to pay the extra expense Fisi would seek.

Duma found himself pulled down under a small white house into a foul smelling, cellar-like room with a dirt floor, where he was promptly chained to a large pillar and left alone in the dark, save for one sliver of light slicing through a narrow opening in the rear wall. It was after he had gotten over his immediate fear that he heard it, the strangest sound imaginable. It wasn't a beast, but whatever it was, made a steady roar-like sound, more soothing than the lion, almost like primal music, over and over, and without ceasing. Duma had, for the first time in his young life, heard the ocean waves ending their long journey from India or Malay, crashing in death upon the coralline rocks of Zanzibar. It would be the sound of the waves dying that at last lulled him to sweet sleep where he could lose, for a moment, the terrible strain of the events that had brought him here.

Stone Town was the capital of the Omani Arab Sultanate, the center of trade and of wealth creation. A fascinating place: with white walled buildings, complete with their ornate patterns; wooden verandas; fortressed wood and iron doors, scattered randomly among narrow winding streets. The famed slave market was in the center of the old town, where slaves, in the most humiliating manner possible, were prodded and inspected by cautious buyers as if they were tired old camels.

The streets of Stone Town were always alive with the bustle of merchants preparing their wares: spice from Pemba Island, including cloves, cinnamon, pepper, and nutmeg, as well as coconuts, cotton cloth from India, gold, tea, coffee, sugar, and other goods from Persia. And, not to be ignored, the African slaves for the harems and fields of the world.

Duma awoke the next morning, startled by the abrupt opening of the heavy cellar door coupled with the rush of blinding light and Arabic speaking voices. It was Fisi that entered and removed his chains from the pillar, that he might be yanked and pulled through the narrow alleys of Stone Town in search of a buyer. Duma thought long and hard of his oath to be the freest slave of all, and his soul was prepared for whatever might befall him.

Fisi had a plan to approach anyone appearing to have wealth with his prize. He had worked too long and hard with the ivory caravan not to be rewarded for his efforts. It was a matter of fate that Fisi's path would take them directly through the very the slave market where Duma's brother Mlima was to be sold that day. Duma's eyes frantically scanned the cluster of slaves huddled like frightened cattle under the building overhang; gaunt black bodies entwined in one mass of flesh, bone, and metal chain. There, in the center, was Mlima. Even sitting, he was taller than the others. Duma started to call out to him, but Mlima never had a chance to hear him because of the interruption created by a pair of magnificent Arabian horses that came galloping down the narrow street and sent people rushing for safety. It was the Sultan's men seeking prime slaves to obtain for Sayyid Majid bin Sa'id. Majid had the honor of being the first Sultan of Zanzibar after his father died, splitting the Omani Sultanate in two.

There was no skirmish, no resistance, just a gold ringed finger pointing at select slaves. Among them was a choice selection, the largest and strongest looking of the lot. It was Mlima, purchased with the transfer of a couple of porcelain-like cowry shells, who would now be spared the drudgery of the spice fields only to eventually become the personal body guard of the Sultan, Sayyid Majid bin Sa'id.

Fisi began to impatiently tug at Duma's chains, but not before Duma had learned the fate of his brother and had felt the deep remorse of not being taken with him. But, that would not be. Duma understood at that moment, that he would never see his brother again.

Fisi's enthusiasm and ivory-laden smile waned slowly as the sun moved through the equatorial sky, apparently unconcerned about the human drama below. Buyer after buyer saw no extra value in a slave that could carve ivory. The reality was that most potential slave buyers thought Duma too small of a man to be of much value for the hard labor they intended. Just as it appeared to be a bad investment of time and effort for Fisi, George Cheney and his wife Sarah appeared in the marketplace with their two small children. They were the perfect couple to approach for the sale. Their clothes and light skin immediately marked them as

Americans, probably Christians and as such, since the signing of the Moresby Treaty with the British; it was illegal to sell a slave to them. Such things as legality seldom bothered the slave traders who regularly found ways around such laws. Fisi was an old hand at circumventing any rule that got in his way.

Confronting the couple with his best ivory-toothed grin he began to ply his trade. "*Maamkio*," he greeted them with the traditional Swahili greeting, while making the humblest of apologies for interrupting such "dignified" people. Surely they had a moment to hear of his personal treasure; a slave who was more valuable than any other in Zanzibar.

George waved the little man aside and began to walk around the repulsive merchant of flesh, having no desire for a slave, as he had already the benefit of two house boys. It was Sarah who noticed the ivory necklace in his hand.

"George, wait just a minute dear," she implored him. "I'd like to see that necklace."

Fisi had planned well. There was value in Duma's carving talent, to stop a buyer long enough to chat. With Fisi, if he could get them to chat, they would usually buy. It was then only a matter of haggling about the price, a custom well practiced in Zanzibar among all of the merchants.

"It's beautiful," Sarah said, "I would really like to buy it, George."

Fisi knew he was at a crossroads. If he pushed too hard, he might lose the sale. If he weakened and sold just the necklace, his only proof of his slave's extra value, he would lose his investment of time and money. He swallowed hard, and flashed his discolored ivory teeth even larger than before. "I'm afraid it's not for sale without its wondrous maker, my Lady." It was the right approach because hearing this awoke immediate passions in George Cheney; a man who made his lucrative livelihood by buying and selling things. Was he not one of the most prominent buyers of ivory in Zanzibar? Who was this small crude man with the awful teeth to tell him that there was something that can't be bought? Fisi's gamble paid off.

The negotiations lasted but a few moments, George had almost convinced Fisi to sell the necklace when Sarah suddenly realized that this young man standing with chains on his wrists was the very one who had carved the beautiful necklace. "*What an opportunity*," she thought, "*to be able to find a slave with such talent.*" Fisi couldn't believe his luck when the success of the sale suddenly shifted to Sarah who pressed her husband with that rapid series of questions that always overwhelmed and caused him to give in.

"Why couldn't we get the slave too? He could make carvings as gifts for my friends back home. I could learn how to carve from him, George; we have all that old ivory lying around. Please dear, this one time?"

It was a simple thing after that; the negotiation of price, and the understanding that Fisi wasn't selling them a slave after all, but was just receiving the two cowries for providing them with an artisan, a "*fundi*," a master craftsman, as a service.

Duma, wondered at the scene as it unfolded before his eyes. He saw the banter, his necklace being displayed, and the woman's interest when she realized it was he who made it. Was this the evil that he feared, to be sold, or did he just escape the drudgery of the field worker forever? If he was to be sold to these strange light-skinned people, he would resign himself to being their property and would work hard, but he would be a slave that was free inside, like that serpent with the red eyes, even if they beat him daily. They could purchase his body but not his spirit.

Surprisingly for Duma, leaving Fisi behind was just a bit threatening for a moment. Wasn't Fisi, with his putrid hyena-like grin, his only connection to his homeland? For an instant he hoped that he might follow Fisi back into the interior to his home near Lake Tanganyika, but it was gone; like his family; like his village, forever.

As he followed the Cheneys through the winding narrow alleyways, he thought, *"What strange masters are they, not even holding his chain? Don't they know how fast Duma can run?"* He made no effort to run, however. It would be of little use in this unfamiliar place, so he resigned himself to follow the strange family in front of him wherever they would go; the man smoking a white meerschaum pipe, the woman clutching his necklace in her hand as if she had found gold, and two small children walking behind them, turning constantly and looking curiously at the shackled Duma. It wasn't until the woman stopped to buy fruit to give him from a street merchant that he first began to realize how lucky he was. Indeed, fate had looked kindly on him that day, for he would never again feel the sting of the whip, nor the cutting weight of chains, unlike so many other poor souls that carried the precious ivory out from the interior of Tanganyika.

CHAPTER FIVE
The serpent cane

I T WASN'T QUITE like the Sultan's palace that Duma's brother, Mlima, had inherited, but to Duma, having never lived in anything other than an earthen floored hut, the Cheney's home was like living in a palace. He was mystified by the tile floors and the upstairs wooden veranda where he could view the magnificent blue ocean in all its splendor and fury. Freed of his chains, he could now move about without worry and he soon began to feel comfortable, certainly more comfortable than he had been made to feel under the weight of that ivory tusk that he and Mlima carried across much of Tanganyika.

He began to realize that, unlike Amri and Faraji, the two houseboys who served the Cheney family's every need; he was afforded a higher status due to his talent for carving, but it was always understood that he was never to assume equality with his owners. Equality was out, but an unspoken respect for both the slave and the Cheney family developed; a mutual respect that surprised both Duma and the Cheney's, especially Sarah and the children, who delighted in watching this unsophisticated young man turn odd pieces of ivory into simple works of art with the crudest of tools.

Duma, in turn, was delighted to be able to talk in Swahili, not only to Amri and Faraji, but the Cheneys also had more than a little understanding of the common language used on the African coast; it was a combination of Arabic and Bantu, with an occasional Persian word or two thrown in for good measure.

His first few days at the Cheney's were spent telling of his life near Lake Tanganyika; though he avoided talking about his capture and the slavers' raid on his small village. Mrs. Cheney was particularly interested in his ivory carving, and she explained that his job was to carve and to teach her the fundamentals of carving ivory.

Duma had his own woven straw mat to sleep on in the far room with Amri and Faraji, and he spent the first few nights awake until the stars filled the sky, just talking with them. He was surprised to find that they had been born and raised on Zanzibar Island, and sold as youngsters to a rich merchant who gifted them to the Cheneys. They, in turn, delighted in his tales of hunting antelope and hartebeests, and actually squealed with delight when he told the story of the time he was chased up a tree by a herd of Cape Buffalo, forced to spend the night in the tree, afraid to come down because the lions and hyena's were prowling for meat.

For the first time since Duma was captured and enslaved, he felt somewhat like a human being again.

His moment of comfort was short lived, however, as he was soon reminded of the slave market and of his brother taken away by Sayyid Majid bin Sa'id's horsemen. He had been with the Cheneys several months when he overheard the Cheneys discuss the Sultan with a guest, an Arab merchant of some sort. There was a comment or two of complaint about their ivory trade being dependent upon the Sultan's approval and that "Sultan Majid controlled everything on Zanzibar; the ivory trade, the spice trade, and the slave trade." They were talking in Duma's own

Swahili as they often did with their visitors and with Duma and the houseboys in an attempt to further their perfection of the local language.

Duma slowly began to piece it together; the ivory, the slave market, the Arabian architecture, and lastly, those men on horseback who took Mlima to serve at the Sultan's palace. He wondered painfully about the fate of his beloved brother. Was Mlima a slave of the sultan now? Was the separation of loved ones, never knowing their fate, an agony that would never be resolved?

Sarah Cheney had arranged for Duma to carve pieces of ivory that were often rejected as imperfect for sale, and ended up stored in the cellar of their home in Zanzibar. Though they were usually odd pieces of discolored or broken tusks; they provided Duma with sufficient material to pursue his carving. Duma's craftsmanship was severely limited by his lack of having the proper tools which prevented him from doing his best work.

It was nearly six months after Duma first came to live with the Cheneys that the shipment from the US arrived in Zanzibar. Sarah had sent a letter to the Pratt ivory shop in Deep River, Connecticut, purchasing for herself and Duma, twin sets of ivory carving tools, the finest available, and in the hands of a skilled carver such as Duma, would allow him complete control over his work.

Duma would remember that day forever. He was resting from carving and had set his work in on a board for the sun to bleach white when Sarah approached him with something hidden behind her back.

"I have something for you Duma," she said rather awkwardly, "for the ivory," she hesitated, "It's from America."

Duma had no idea what "America" was, but he could tell by her manner that she was a bit uncomfortable and his heart raced for the briefest moment as he feared that she had come to tell him he was to be sold again. He had already begun to relax in the

Cheney's home and had found great joy in being able to live his life free to carve what he wished in the ivory.

Sarah slowly unwrapped the thick waxed cloth and carefully exposed one tool after another: chisels, reams, tiny saws with tiny teeth, awls, and other more specialized implements of steel; tools that were instantly recognizable as being useful in the ivory carving business. She looked intently at his face for a reaction. Duma's heart fluttered rapidly when he realized that his master had just given him a *zawadi*, a gift for himself; it was, next to his freedom, the finest gift possible.

Sarah was deeply disappointed that Duma had failed to thank her, as he merely reached out and took the package of tools, putting them on the wooden veranda floor where he had been doing his work. Turning his back to her, he sat down and began to feel the sharp edges to verify their quality. Sarah turned and went back into the house wondering if she had made a mistake, expecting manners from a slave.

Sitting at her reading desk a week later, Sarah was now feeling badly for worrying about silly things such as Duma's manners, when she heard a knock on her door. Duma entered, with a broad smile, his hands behind his back, clasping a partially hidden piece of white ivory which he displayed at her urging. It was a marvelous piece of ivory, a comb-like hairpiece decorated with an intricate procession of cheetahs running across the top. The teeth of the piece were of such precision that one might suspect that a machine had done the work. On the very edge of the comb, Sarah could just make out the paw print of a cheetah. He smiled broadly, for he too had now given her a zawadi, as was the custom in his village.

She decided then to teach Duma, along with her own two children, to read and write English, even though such an act as educating a slave was frowned upon. This Duma she had found in the marketplace was far more than a mere slave. Never again would she think of him as such, for he was a unique person with rare talent, a keen mind and a human heart; something the slavers would deny to the end.

Duma soon became a constant companion to Sarah, who would take him with her to the markets, always being careful to avoid the slave market area of Stone Town. He would gladly carry the goods and the various fruits that she purchased, often enjoying with her the beautiful bold patterns on the hand-made cotton textiles from strange far off places. Duma once asked her what the pungent, but beautiful, scent of cloves was that sometimes permeated the usually foul Zanzibar air, but she declined to discuss the spice trade with him, very aware that such luxuries were only afforded by enslaving black people. She was apparently not as keenly aware about the cruelty surrounding the ivory business that had brought her and her husband to Zanzibar.

It was during one of these market excursions with "Mwana," as Duma had respectably taken to addressing Sarah, that he once again encountered the Sultan's horsemen. If there ever were careless horsemen, it would be those of the Sultan Majid. Duma recognized them instantly as he rounded a corner near the British consulate with Mrs. Cheney. Once again, he was forced to press his back up against the white building, and once again, he felt his heart pounding in his chest as the Sultan's horses pushed by him and Sarah Cheney, and galloped down the narrow street.

"Majid is a mighty Sultan, but his horsemen could well use some manners, she complained, brushing herself off.

"Who is Majid?" Duma asked in Swahili.

He is the Sultan; he lives in that palace over by the big garden, Duma, and those are his men who nearly trampled us."

"I have never seen the palace," he said. "Is it beautiful?"

"Yes it is Duma,"

"Are there slaves there?"

Sarah caught her breath. She was not prepared to deal directly with the right or wrong of slavery with Duma, though she was personally appalled at the treatment afforded most of the slaves. Wasn't the same slave culture at work back in America? George and she had often discussed the idea that this was, unfortunately, the culture that existed in Zanzibar, and there was little they could do to change it. Neither of them ever connected their ivory purchasing business to the slave trade; except, to convince themselves that if they didn't trade in ivory, someone else would, hardly realizing that such self-serving arguments merely allow people to continue to do what they know deep inside is wrong.

"Yes Duma, there are slaves there," she reluctantly responded, waiting nervously for his next question. It never came, for Duma knew the answers to those kinds of questions already.

After that, Duma began to ponder more and more the fate of his brother and the other slaves. Eventually he began to feel guilty for having such a free life when other slaves were suffering so.

I must speak through my carving about this evil," he thought. It was then that he remembered the snake. That serpent would soon become his free soul carved in ivory.

Duma began searching under the Cheney house for the right piece of ivory to make his symbol of freedom, but found only partial pieces of tusk to use. There would be no large prime ivory for his serpents. This caused him to be depressed and forlorn for a few weeks. Mrs. Cheney noticed the change in his personality and confronted him one day asking him why he was so unhappy in her house, but he just smiled weakly and kept the real reason to himself.

The solution to Duma's problem came soon enough. It happened one evening, just after the Cheneys had finished their evening meal of guinea fowl. Duma had noticed Amri lifting the carcass of the bird as he started to clean the table.

"How foolish of me," he thought, *"if I can't find a whole tusk of ivory to make my serpent, I'll build one from smaller pieces, the same way that this bird was created by its maker."*

That evening, he set about gathering pieces of ivory, taking care to match the color and size of each piece. Like the bird's wings and legs, he would make holes in one piece and fit the next one to it tightly, so that it may appear as one large piece. *"I shall make it so well that only the serpent and I will know that it was formed from small pieces."*

An old man selling pottery in the market gave Duma the answer to the final problem he had. The serpent would be his design theme, but it must be carved on something practical. Art, to Duma, had to be both beautiful and useful. The old man stood up to show Sarah Cheney a bowl that he had crafted. She had asked for a low, flat one for flouring fish; it was in the back of his display. Duma noticed the man's missing foot as he walked back to get the bowl; a teakwood cane was his second leg.

"He is free to move just as the serpent was free, only because of his cane," or as Duma called it in Swahili; a *fimbo.*

Duma decided then that he would construct and carve an ivory fimbo with two entwined serpents on it; one representing Duma, and one for Mlima, so that they may both become free. It would become the finest cane ever carved.

CHAPTER SIX
At the palace, life and death

ENSLAVED AT THE sultan's palace, Mlima stood several hands taller than anyone and soon began to recover his lost strength. Unlike Duma, his method of escape from the harsh reality of his enslavement was to become the strongest slave around. He loved to carry heavy things that would require two other slaves to lift. If there was an impossible task to be done, it would be Mlima that would be called to lift, break, or move the unachievable. He always succeeded, gaining the respect and cheers of the others. For the giant that he was, Mlima was also a very pleasant man who was liked by all as he settled quickly into his new life as a palace slave.

Sultan Majid bin Sa'id was the most powerful man in Zanzibar and was known far and wide for his wealth and cunning, but any man that powerful, always has enemies. In Majid's case, there were few, but he did have one dangerous man who might wish to see him deposed, if not dead, his brother, Thuwaini bin Sa'id. They had been at odds ever since their famous father, Sa'id ibn Sultan died and left the great Omani Sultanate for their inheritance. A personal dispute arose, causing them to split the sultanate in two; one part, Thuwaini bin Sultan would control in Oman, and the other part; the far wealthier Zanzibar, would be ruled by Majid.

Fearing that Thuwaini bin Sa'id would not rest until he also took control of Zanzibar and its vast wealth, Majid demanded nothing but the finest protection, including his personal garrison of guards. But that was not enough for Majid. Feeling that few of the guards could be trusted with his life, he would also need the strongest and most loyal man to be his personal bodyguard. When he heard of the palace reputation of Mlima, "a giant, with the body as strong as a two big men," he decided to act; he summoned Mlima to his chamber one day.

Mlima felt uncomfortably like displayed merchandise standing in the Sultan's private chamber. Majid slowly walked around his massive body. Mlima's shimmering dark skin was to be envied, and his powerful muscles admired. The Sultan knew that he could never be strong like Mlima, but he would have no need to, as he already owned this powerful man. Now he must make this Mlima, who could easily tear him in two with his bare hands, his most trustworthy servant, even to the point of dying for him, if need be. Mlima was strong, but not more than Majid was cunning. If he was ever to be able to entirely trust his own bodyguard; he must give that bodyguard a solid reason to be loyal and dedicated to him.

"When I die, you shall become a free man, if you serve me well," he began. "You will be the servant of no one, but me. You will be free from the lash and the pillar and I will give you my best scimitar from Persia to use in my defense. Unless I send you outside my chamber, you will always follow me, as close as the tail follows the lion, never leaving my side. Do you understand?"

Mlima was overwhelmed. He had not gotten past hearing about his chance at freedom when he began to deeply wish that his moistened eyes would not be detected and weaken his chance to be the Sultan's personal protector.

"Yes Sayyid, It would be my honor to protect you with my life. I will be forever grateful," he replied, in his most humble Swahili.

"This is to be then. You may call me Majid, and I shall call you as you are, *Baba*, my mountain." Thenceforth, around the palace, Mlima quickly became known as el Baba, the protector.

The greatest thrill of el Baba's new life was in being present when the Sultan greeted important visitors and merchants from around the world, especially the British Consul, Lieutenant Trevor Sutherland, who seemed to be discussing the slave trade regularly with Majid. The Consulate had been created to help enforce the Moresby Treaty, wherein, the British had successfully pressured Majid's father to agree that no slaves could be sold to western Christians. It was a poorly enforced treaty in reality. Nonetheless, the British were constantly trying to bring a halt to the slave business in East Africa, an effort that often produced little more than cosmetic results. It was always understood, though, that it would do neither side any good to arouse too much anger; thus, both the Consul Southerland and Sultan Majid managed to remain rather respectful of each other's business needs.

It was not always peaceful in the palace. The center of wealth often became the center of controversy. El Baba had hardy had a chance to become familiar with his responsibility of protecting Majid when a threat to Majid's very life occurred. It started rather quietly with a discussion between an Asian merchant and Majid about an ivory shipment to Malay and then it progressed into a more openly hostile dispute, making el Baba immediately nervous as to his proper role. The Malaysian merchant, who felt he had been lied to about the quality of an ivory shipment, and thus, having suffered a loss of sufficient wealth, demanded retribution in the form of money and an apology to mend his damaged pride. When Majid laughed at such an absurd demand, the merchant pulled a pistol from under his jacket and fired point blank range at Majid, but not before el Baba had moved quickly into the very path of the bullet, sending the little man backwards, breaking his neck with the force of a powerful blow. The primer powder flashed brilliantly, but the gun which had fortunately misfired, caused no damage to either Majid or el Baba.

Majid, astounded by el Baba's display of willingness to die for him, offered him any gift that he chose from the palace treasury, but el Baba graciously declined.

"It is yours to chose whenever you wish el Baba," said Majid, "for you have served me well." It was an offer that would change future events in ways that neither man could imagine at the time.

CHAPTER SEVEN
What is this America?

MANY MONTHS HAD passed since Duma first began carving the serpent cane and many nights he found himself polishing and buffing it out on the veranda by moonlight. Every moment that he wasn't teaching Sarah how to carve, making a special trinket for her family and friends in America, or going into Stone Town with her, was spent carving, sawing, cutting, or piecing together his beloved fimbo, his guarantee of freedom for Mlima's and his own spirits. He would accept nothing but perfection in his treasure, often dismantling pieces and carving them again, always seeking to make it the best fimbo ever.

Duma spent other times together with Mrs. Cheney. She too, had a project that would not rest until it was complete, teaching Duma how to read and write English, Duma was a willing student, but was confused as to why he needed to learn such a language when they already understood everyone in Zanzibar, who usually spoke Swahili. Had he had the ability to know his future, he would have tried even harder to learn the new language.

Duma's preferred language however, was the language of

carving, and no one spoke it better than he did, particularly, when he finally finished the cane. At first, he was going to keep it private and not show the Cheneys the cane, though all of the Cheneys had watched him many times working on various parts of the serpents. Duma had even shown Sarah how to carve the intricate scales of a reptile, and make row after row of the subtle glowing texture that only ivory can produce. Sarah, for her part, had created a small lizard showing the skill of a good beginning craftsman. It was Duma's pride that finally helped persuade him to share his treasure with the Cheneys, partly because he knew that what he made really belonged to them, and partly because he needed something of value from them to finish it off correctly. The serpent he saw had red eyes; the kind that could be represented by the red glass beads that Mrs. Cheney often used as money in the marketplace. The problem for Duma was this: could he, a slave, expect to receive money from his masters?

There was only one way he could finish the cane properly and that was to tell them that this extra cost was but part of a gift to both of them. He had no problem with not owning the cane; it was only important that it be made to free forever the spirits of both he and his brother. He decided to approach Mrs. Cheney with the cane when she was alone.

"I have a gift for you Mrs. Cheney," he boldly said in English, surprising Sarah even more than he had with the comb he had carved for her. She looked at the cane across his open palms and marveled at what she saw.

"Even the master carvers of Asia would admire this," she told Duma, then noticing the concave holes, where the serpents' eyes should be, she remarked, "But is it not yet finished Duma?"

"The serpents' eyes must be red, like your beads," his eyes dropped to the floor in expectation of certain retribution for daring such boldness.

"Oh dear," she replied when she realized his request. "But, those beads would purchase much in the marketplace."

He smiled bravely, hiding his hurt as he placed the ivory cane in her hands. Duma turned and abruptly left, before the inner pain removed his smile.

Sarah's problem wasn't with Duma's request. It was with how she could justify it to her husband, who would certainly see the beads and know what had transpired without his permission.

That evening she waited until after George Cheney had finished his cup of gin, and then brought up the subject; she wisely left the decision to him, but not without first pressuring him with the tone of her request. He asked to see the cane and he also was taken aback by its rare beauty.

"That's quite a slave we have bought for ourselves Sarah!" he exclaimed.

"He's not our slave, George."

She reminded him that Duma had become her good companion and carving teacher and that he had learned much of the English language already and, finally, she played the trump card, "Westerners, Dear, cannot own slaves."

"You would think, by the manner in which you're teaching him to read and write all the time my dearest Sarah, that you intend to take Duma back to New England with us when we leave this fall."

Sarah had not really thought about what would happen to Duma when they returned home to America, but she knew that she could never leave him here in Zanzibar to live the horrible fate of a slave.

"With your permission, of course, George, that is exactly what I intend to do," she retorted, surprising even herself with her certainty of mission.

George Cheney slumped deeper in his chair, confronted with an impossible choice; to cause a serious divide between him and the woman he loved, or to bring a slave back to America, just as a war involving slavery was breaking out there. He poured himself another drink.

That night Sarah slipped into Duma's room and left the cane and four red beads on the floor next to his mat while he was sleeping. Duma breathed a long sigh as he watched her quietly leave the room.

The next morning George and Sarah told Duma that they would all be going to home to America.

"What is America?" he asked in English, for he had heard the word many times, not knowing what it meant. Then followed a long discussion about America, the slavery issue and that they would be leaving Zanzibar soon, taking Duma with them. They had agreed not to tell Duma, until they were on the ship, that he would arrive in America as a free man.

George Cheney then surprised both Sarah and Duma when he announced that he was now to be the new sole owner of the cane and that he fully intended to give it away. The trade had been made, Duma's freedom for the cane. George Cheney was not a man without motives.

The last few months in Zanzibar passed quickly for the Cheney family and Duma. Preparation for the voyage with the help of the two houseboys, Amri and Faraji, was rather easy. They would soon be staying in Zanzibar as houseboys at the British Consulate; it would insure their eventual freedom. The last order of business for George Cheney was to provide for a secure and permanent source of quality ivory for the ivory processing plants in Connecticut, one of which would one day carry the name of Cheney on its facade.

CHAPTER EIGHT
The gift

GEORGE CHENEY HAD been to the Sultan's palace many times in the decade that he lived as an ivory merchant in Zanzibar. He had a good relationship with both, Majid's father, Sa'id bin Sultan and, his son, Majid bin Sultan and he intended to use it to his advantage in his present and final mission.

Clutching the ivory cane, with its four red imbedded eyes, he approached the Sultan graciously when his name was announced. Majid knew that the Cheneys were leaving Zanzibar soon, and he expected this courtesy call. What he didn't expect, however, was the magnificent ivory cane as a gift.

"Where did you get such a fine work of art?" he asked the well known ivory merchant. He immediately clutched the cane tightly to his breast, lest someone attempt to take it away.

"From the ivory gods, where else?" Cheney jested, "Nothing less for Sayyid Majid."

To say that Majid was pleased, would be to understate his appreciation. The sultan was a powerful man, but not a fool. Nothing in Zanzibar of any value was ever exchanged without a price. He would now find out what the price of such a valuable gift as this cane would be.

"And what is expected of this Sultan, for receiving such a fine gift?" he asked, searching George Cheney's face for an answer.

"It is merely in appreciation for allowing me the opportunity of purchasing the finest of the ivory in Zanzibar these past years."

Majid still didn't get the answer he wanted, and continued to play the game of seeking the real motive behind George Cheney's gift.

"And…?" He let the question hang in the palace air like the scent of cloves from Pemba, demanding now some truthful reaction.

"That Majid would be so kind to as to insure that the finest ivory continues to be sent to America would be sufficient appreciation, Sayyid," he said, finally conceding some truth as to why he brought the gift.

"That is all, Mr. Cheney, nothing else?"

"There is one small thing Sayyid."

"Yes, what is it?" replied the Sultan, long ago expecting such roundabout banter to occur in this world of tradesmen.

"I have a boy that I would like to take back to America with Sarah and the children."

"We have a treaty with our friends the British as you know," smiled the Sultan, now knowing the full reason for the visit and the gift.

"But Majid, are you not the great Sultan?" George Cheney knew the proper words to say.

Majid thought a bit. This, for him, was no problem, but he relished having the power to decide. There was no point in having power unless you exercised it properly, and that meant that all such decisions must appear difficult, as if great wisdom were required for each one. Finally, he spoke. "Your boy will be a worker assigned to the ship when you arrive at the dock to board the ship. You may do with him what you please in America."

"And the ivory?"

Majid knew that America was rapidly becoming one of the biggest participants in the ivory business, and he had no desire to risk losing that market.

"Your cane is a most gracious gift. You will have all the best ivory you wish for your America."

George Cheney, having no need to continue their ritual, thanked Majid profusely and retreated from the palace. He achieved what he came for, but he missed entirely what would occur next.

Majid turned to el Baba, who had watched many times, this game of giving gifts to the Sultan for a favor, and, as required, he had always done so in an apparently disinterested manner.

"Take this with care el Baba; it is of great value to me."

El Baba scooped the precious artwork into his massive hands, and instantly admired its captivating beauty. Something deep inside urged him to examine it more closely. Turning it over carefully several times, he was about to dismiss his curiosity; then he saw it, the small paw print of the cheetah engraved under one of the serpent's heads. *"Duma! It was he who had made it. He was alive and apparently well enough to create such a masterpiece."*

Once again, this giant man's eyes moistened with passion. He had heard the conversation with George Cheney only too well. It would be his brother Duma that would be leaving for America with the ivory trader.

Later that month, a lone young black man from the interior of Tanganyika, stood near the bow of a clipper heading west around the southern tip of the African continent; he was playing like a child with a long piece of hemp that had a heavy knot tied on the end. Duma leaned against the ship's railing, raised the ball of hemp and dropped it; it touched only chosen waves. Like the serpent that was free, he decided with great care which waves he would touch and which waves he would not. Earlier that same morning, the Cheneys had told him he was now a free man and he would live as such, in America.

CHAPTER NINE
To challenge the Sultan

E VER SO SLOWLY, the movements to abolish slavery in the West began to creep across the oceans and across Africa to affect even the mighty Sultans in their not so humble palaces. In Zanzibar, Majid was beginning to no longer relish a visit from the British Consul, Lieutenant Southerland, who under pressure from Parliament back home, began to use increasing threats of force against Majid. The slave trade, with its myriad of connections to vast international merchants was not about to go quietly, but the disruption of the consciences of too many in the West began to take its inevitable toll. Toward the end of Majid's reign; the inescapable confrontation between the British Consul and the Sultan had reached the boiling point.

"We no longer can accept the situation where Dhows stuffed full of black slaves leave Zanzibar to be shipped around the earth's seas for your profit," a furious British officer informed Majid."

"And what would you have me do Lieutenant, start a war over your problem? There are simply too many threads in this mat of slavery. If I pull but one, the entire mat will unravel."

"British gunships will not continue forever to protect Zanzibar if it means protecting the trading of slaves Majid," he warned.

Consul Southerland realized that Majid spoke some truth. Something as large as the entire East African slave trade with all its entrenched tentacles of power and wealth throughout the world, couldn't, stop suddenly without serious conflict. Like all men involved with making such potentially dangerous decisions, Trevor Southerland, chose not to push too far, lest an unstoppable crisis develop. Things, however, could no longer exist without some significant change. He tried a new tact, anything to get the pressure from back home off of his back.

"I need some evidence to show Parliament, something concrete, something to buy you time to do what you must eventually do, Majid. Stop the slave trade."

Once again, Majid slipped into his façade of the wise thinker, and he pretended to agonize over a great decision, a decision he had no intention of making just yet. If he could dismiss this problem with a few baubles he would, but this was bigger and would take some measure of capitulation on his part. At last he sighed, and then spoke.

"I will have my men show you where the slaves are loaded into the dhows at night. You will make a raid, perhaps, for your glory back home. I can do no more," he said, as he moved his hand in a motion to dismiss the Consul.

The young officer realized that he needed much more. They had previously intercepted slaves as they were being shipped, and Majid would just have the workers load the slave dhows somewhere else. This would not do. He ignored the dismissal.

El Baba and the two guards at the door took immediate notice of Southerland's bold challenge and instantly prepared to enforce, by any means, the Sultan's decision to dismiss the Consul. The Sultan's wishes were, after all, the Sultan's wishes, and not to be treated lightly.

The decision to confront the entire British Empire was too much to risk, even for a man as powerful as Majid. An incident of this nature with the Consul now would turn his British protectors into his immediate enemy and he knew it.

Looking at the massive muscular back of el Baba, who had now moved between the Sultan and the threatening officer, he had an idea. "You are indeed correct Lieutenant Southerland," he began, "I shall give you what you need to quiet the storm in your house of Parliament. You shall offer them a gift as proof of my good intentions on your behalf. I will send, to your parliament, two ships of one hundred slaves each that I will set free at no cost as evidence that I am tightening the noose on slavery," then without hesitation, he continued fattening the sacrificial offer.

"I'll give to you personally, my beloved bodyguard, el Baba, to have as certain evidence of my most gracious willingness to work with you on this problem of slavery that we all have to deal with." And then knowing he had given more than expected, and by so doing bought more time to continue the slave trade as he wished, he waved the Counsel away. The officer rigidly stood his ground.

El Baba whirled around to face the Sultan that he that had learned to accept as his master. He had understood clearly that he was now to be this British officer's property and was torn as to his proper duty. *"To which man do I belong? Which man must I protect from the other?"*

It took a few moments for Trevor Southerland to realize what had just transpired. He now had what he needed, a prize to take back to Parliament as a victory of sorts, and the personal joy of having gained the freedom of hundreds of poor souls by just allowing himself to finally get sufficiently angry about the situation. He would accept Majid's offer; though, he knew that the encounter was but a pause in the ongoing conflict surrounding East African slavery. He also knew that he couldn't bring anything other than free men back to the British Isles.

Turning to the huge man that Majid had just freed, he asked, "Are you ready for your new home, el Baba?"

Mlima, or el Baba, or whoever he was, was frightened and

confused. He was torn between two forces: the security of staying with Majid here in the palace, and the sheer joy of being free, and going away with this British officer to an unknown place far away as had his brother Duma.

He really had no choice. He was simply property that had just been given to another. There was, however, one thing that must still be done.

"I cannot go Sayyid," he heard himself say.

Majid leaned forward, and grasped the arms of his chair in astonishment. Neither Majid nor the Consul could believe what this titan of a man had just said. It was never acceptable for a slave, no matter how large and powerful, to express open disagreement with so mighty man as Majid. None before him had ever dared!

"Your gracious Sultan has honored me by allowing me to become his humble servant and I have served you well. Have I not done just that?" el Baba asked.

Majid settled back in his chair thinking, *"My loyal slave was just paying homage to me, and he now hopes to stay with me here in the palace."*

"I have given him my word. You are free el Baba. Go with him," he smiled faintly.

"There is still a promise for you to keep, my Sayyid," he spoke more softly now. "The ivory serpent cane; you assured my choice...."

"Your freedom is your promised treasure el Baba," said Majid, cutting him off, as the smile slipped from his face.

"But Sayyid, what is the value of your word?"

"Go, before I change my mind!" said Majid, growing angrier at the thought that a slave should dare to challenge him."

"What is this about a serpent cane Majid?" asked the young officer, sensing the importance of it, "that a slave would risk his freedom or his life for it?"

Before Majid could respond, el Baba in frustration, standing even taller and more certain of his position said, "For risking my life to save him, he promised me …"

"Enough, it is not to be!" Majid was also standing now, while the two palace guards moved in quickly.

"So," said the officer boldly advancing even closer to the Sultan, "you expected me a moment ago to tell Parliament that the Sultan of Zanzibar's word to stop slavery is as pure as the finest pearl, but now you choose instead to require me to tell them that your word is but nothing more than the vaporized stench of a cesspool?"

Majid was fuming. His cunning mind raced for a way out, but there was only one. He turned and motioned to his guards who, mistaking his gesture, reached for their swords. The officer too reached for his pistol.

Majid, capitulating, put his hands up to insure that there was to be no violence, turned to the guards, and told them, through his clenched teeth, "Remove your presence to my treasury and bring the serpent fimba to me."

Moments later, through the palace gate came a smiling British officer and a very large black man clutching an ivory cane with serpents gracing its exterior. To el Baba, its real value was the small cheetah print under one of the two serpents' heads. He would soon add his mountain mark under the other serpent's head. Now Duma and he would both be free.

CHAPTER TEN
Ivory and the long tidal river

IT STARTED OUT as pure Yankee craftsmanship that turned crude stained ivory tusks into things of beauty and function. The Industrial Revolution, however, caused it to change from a rather simple, if not cumbersome trade enjoyed by a few skilled men, into the roaring business that made the lower Connecticut River the final resting place on the journey of one of the world's most precious commodities - Ivory. Who could have predicted that the name of a New England town, created solely for the purposes of processing ivory, and many thousands of miles away from the nearest wild elephant, would be named after the common name for elephant teeth?

Ivoryton, Connecticut, and its competitive sister town of Deep River, were the heart of the phenomenon of tusk processing for much of the world during the last half of the nineteenth and the early twentieth century. It began slowly, with everyday nineteenth century commodities made first with bone and then with ivory: combs, buttons and toothpicks, though the major item demanded, from one of the nation's most rapidly growing industries, was pianos, including ivory keys and keyboards.

Once machines were invented to more rapidly process the white gold into things of function, the business of killing elephants in Africa moved into high gear, and that generated ever more need for still more slaves to carry the ivory out of the interior to the trade centers on the Indian Ocean. It was here in 1860, on the peaceful banks of the Connecticut River, that five people arrived from Zanzibar: George A. Cheney, his wife Sarah, their children and a young black man named Duma.

This was a heart-wrenching time in America. The Civil War was about to begin and the issue of slavery was on everyone's mind. There were moral and economic issues to be dealt with, and just several hundred miles south of Connecticut, black slaves, forcibly brought there from the West Coast of Africa, were working the tobacco and cotton fields of the south.

In the islands of the Caribbean and Brazil, slaves brought over from western Africa in the Atlantic Slave Trade, were suffering the pain and indignities of having to produce sugar and molasses for the rum industry. Rum, which had in earlier times been distilled right next door in neighboring Rhode Island, was often used as payment for the purchase of even more slaves from Africa. The rum trade was an industry that, like ivory, would necessitate the continued use of black slave labor, even after the Emancipation Proclamation was signed by Abraham Lincoln, and the last gun in the War Between the States had been laid down.

This appetite for slavery continued out of sight, and therefore, out of the minds of most people in the continental United States. The same nation that would spill its own blood to divorce itself from direct participation in the abuse of enslaved Africans would not yet stop the abuse of those other enslaved Africans, thousands of miles away, whose blood would be spilled because of this nation's thirst for spices and ivory.

That very same Zanzibar Prime Ivory was also in the hold of the ship carrying the Cheneys and Duma to New England. George and Sarah were relieved to be coming back home to settle down here in southern New England, but for Duma, arriving in New England was an extremely unsettling experience.

Any description of Duma's emotions upon seeing the bluffs of Fisher's Island and the Connecticut shore would have to include fear. *"What kind of strange land was this? Why are there no long balmy white sand beaches lined with swaying palm trees, no deep blue seas, or no stunning sunsets,"* he wondered, as the screeching of gulls proudly announced the arrival of his sailing vessel to the narrow sound? He could see land on all sides now: the long soft blue fingers of Long Island to his left and the rather plain solemn Connecticut shore on his right; but most offensive of all, the air rushing into his face was cold and bitter. It was October and the frigid air from Canada had swept down in one of its occasional early assaults upon southern New England, causing households everywhere to begin unpacking wool blankets and clothing in preparation for the winter that was to come. The force of the wind created froth to crust the crests of every wave rolling down the long sound from the direction of New York City.

Duma, although sheltered with George Cheney's heavier wool coat, stood shivering, already hating the cold and fearing his new freedom. How could he survive in such a land with no home or means of gathering food? *"Would the Cheneys leave him like Fisi did?"* He began once more to yearn dearly for his home back in Africa. Even with its hazards, it was at least a familiar environment where an industrious man could survive with simple effort and few rules. If he were truly free; he would be home, hunting on the shores of Lake Tanganyika, but that home was no longer there: it was long ago destroyed by the slavers and the Arab ivory caravans.

The ship turned the corner to enter the mouth of the large river, greeted by a fierce wall of ominous white water. The incoming tide and the northwest wind were savagely whipping the outgoing river current and preventing the ship from sailing the few miles upriver to the shelter of Deep River's harbor. It would have to wait till morning and spend the night anchored safely in the southernmost cove just north of Saybrook Point.

A thin misty cloud cover moving in from the south greeted the ship at dawn. The seas had calmed now as Duma's ship sailed back out into the river, no longer encumbered by walls of oncoming waves. It passed by a New York City bound steamship belching smoke as it plowed its way downstream toward Long Island Sound.

Less than an hour later the seagoing vessel nudged its way up against the town landing docks in Deep River. Already the waterfront was bustling. A few yards south of where Duma stood watching, men were busy hammering galvanized iron nails into the hull frame of a large ship, and a few yards further behind them was a small railroad for launching the newly built ships. Shore hands in dirty aprons and odd shaped hats were already beginning to unload the cargo from those holds in the belly of the ship that were teaming with the lifeblood of this small community, ivory.

Just as when he was thrust suddenly into the bustle of Zanzibar's Stone Town, Duma was subjected to new and wondrous sights. His keen artist's spirit broke through his fears long enough to absorb this new world; he took instant notice of the strangest of trees whose odd autumn leaves were bathed in the bright colors of a Zanzibar sunset. He had never imagined the likes of these odd mountain-shaped roofs pierced by tall brick chimneys on large painted wooden buildings with tiny glass windows. Dominating the scene were several prominent buildings, including a large one made completely of stone. Carts on the dirt street below were already receiving their loads of ivory carried from the bowels of the vessel.

The most intimidating thing of all was that not one man, woman, or child, was without pale white skin. There were no black or brown people to be seen here in this strange land. There was no pungent odor of spices drifting across his nostrils to inhale with delight. Nor were there any chattering dark-skinned merchants in the streets selling trinkets, pottery, fruit, or brightly patterned cotton cloth. But, he also noticed, neither was there a market crowded with emaciated slaves in shackles. Unlike in Africa, only white men were struggling to lift the heavy ivory into the carts. There were no armed guards standing by to insure that their labor continue.

Duma had, for better or worse, come to his final home. This ex-slave would leave his mark on this quaint river town in the most unexpected way.

CHAPTER ELEVEN
What is this strange parchment?

ONNECTICUT LAW WAS clear in that slavery was prohibited. This caused a bit of a problem for the Cheneys. Were they to have Duma stay with them? He would be viewed as a covert slave brought back by them from Zanzibar for housekeeping purposes. He could not even work for George Cheney in the new Comstock Ivoryton plant without creating suspicion. It would just not do to allow any work accomplished, or money earned by Duma, to be in any manner related to the Cheneys. They had discussed this problem and had found a solution even while they were still in Zanzibar. Sarah wrote George Read the co-owner of the ivory shop in Deep River, who surprisingly enough, was an ardent and active abolitionist. George had agreed to accept responsibility for Duma and had already arranged for Duma to board with him and work in the Pratt Read factory with his beloved ivory.

George Read had long ago made a commitment to helping slaves; he had provided shelter for a runaway slave, who, fearful of detection under the Fugitive Slave Act, had changed his name and wore a disguise. "Billy" Winters had come north from the southern plantations, through the Underground Railroad, before the Civil War broke out, and with the help of George Read had taken up residence in an old shack on the edge of town. Keeping to himself at first, Billy proved to be a hard worker. He quickly learned the value of a dollar and began a rigid program of saving every bit of the money he earned by working in the stables and helping transport ivory in the carts for the Pratt Read company.

Billy was a determined man with one major goal; to bring his relatives up North to freedom; a task he was finally able to accomplish after the war ended and emancipation became a reality. Duma and Billy didn't share much more than a neighborly greeting with each other in those early years, and neither managed to discuss their own experiences as slaves.

Duma did have, as expected, a bit more difficulty adjusting to Connecticut than did Billy, never having spent any time in America at all, but he did bring with him the artistic skills, that served him more than well.

Sarah Cheney had been especially careful to bring back Duma's ivory tools; she knew his carving would be valuable to Mr. Read's business. To say that George Read would be well served with such a talented employee would be understating the situation. The Pratt Read Co., in Deep River, had many capable and skilled craftsmen already manufacturing fine ivory products that were in demand, but the one thing that neither the Pratt Read Co., nor the Comstock plant in nearby Ivoryton had, was an artist, a carver of original art for the specialty ivory products they often had requests for.

George Read's first task was to arrange for Duma to be clothed in more traditional clothing sufficient to endure work, and New England winters, and, as such, he had an array of used clothing waiting for Duma to use.

"Shoes?" Duma repeated, in response to Read's urging. "Must I wear them always?"

"Not to bed and sometimes in the summer Duma, otherwise,

yes. The streets and factory will hurt your feet," he patiently advised the young man.

Duma's experiences with this new world of strange clothing was both frustrating and fascinating, particularly two things: tying his shoes and using buttons. At first, he had a lot of difficulty learning to tie a cumbersome bow knot with his shoelaces, but soon marveled how easily such a knot came loose when necessary. His normally nimble fingers fumbled with uncertainty when he tried to button the old cotton shirts that were salvaged from George Read's modest clothing assortment. He thought that it would be much easier just to wrap cotton material around his chest and shoulders as he had done back in Africa.

He had already learned, with the Cheneys back in Zanzibar, to use utensils rather than his fingers, so he had little difficulty at the dinner table. He even enjoyed the strange new foods that he was offered, and quickly developing favorites, such as, the oatmeal and molasses he enjoyed each morning, not yet aware that the molasses he enjoyed, as well as the cotton shirts he wore, came by way of slavery.

The most immediate benefit of the heavyweight wool clothing he received was the cessation of his constant shivering.

"It is not very warm here, Bwana; I like these heavy clothes a lot."

"It will get plenty warm in the summer Duma," said the tender man laughing, "Warmer than you can imagine right now," and then he reminded Duma to always call him Mr. Read, fearful that any Swahili language he used, might be a cause for ridicule from the other factory workers. Duma was unable to fathom the concept of changing seasons, until he remembered that even in equatorial Africa, when he was carrying the ivory tusk across Tanganyika; it was colder on the higher mountains.

Duma's room was surprisingly bright. It had a southeastern exposure and was higher up on a modest hill that overlooked the tidal river where Duma could watch the various activities, and it turned out to be one of Duma's favorite places to escape from reality and to daydream.

Gazing out the window, he was reminded of Zanzibar where he had often noticed the fishermen in their boats tending their nets. He thought, *"How easy it is to catch fish without having to spear them one at a time."* The Connecticut River was home to several fishermen who also plied their trade with nets and were able to catch everything from striped bass to the seasonal runs of that large member of the herring family, the shad.

While Duma spent his time staring at his strange new world, his strange new world was also staring at him. His dark skin was an uncommon sight in Deep River and folks there were well aware of the ongoing war and the slavery issues. They had long known that George Read was an ardent abolitionist who had risked bringing Billy Winters to Connecticut, but in such a small community they also learned that Duma was a free black man from Africa and not a runaway slave from down South. Those who would work with him in the Pratt factory learned this first hand. It was his ivory carving skills that quickly paved the way for that understanding.

He was quite a sight that first day working in the factory. The men, busy as they had been, making buttons, combs, billiard balls and piano keys from ivory tusks, stopped working and stared at the young black man in slightly too-large clothing, standing in the doorway, holding his crude bag of carving tools. A quick admonishment from George Read sent them back to their labor, lest they imperil their precious employment.

There were no formal introductions or tours of the factory to greet Duma. He was led to a well-worn bench with a stool and a window facing the main street and told that this was his place to carve. George knew that Duma was a very skilled carver, for he had seen Sarah Cheney's marvelous hair comb and wondered at its intricate beauty, but he had a special role in mind for Duma to play, a role that would reward both Duma and himself.

His first task would be a grand one, carving custom ivory handles to fit the popular guns made by Sam Colt. Not only was the Colt factory just north up the turnpike in Hartford, but his revolvers were in high demand around the world. Custom ivory handles were desired by the more well-to-do customers who were eager to differentiate their Colt's from all others. If Read guessed right, there would be a lucrative market for handcrafted, one-of-a-kind, revolver handles. For Duma, it would be just a matter of selecting prime ivory, carving a different design or scene in each and learning to fit the pieces properly.

Within a couple of hours after arriving at Phineas Pratt's factory, Duma was already attracting attention; the workers and the managers alike managed to slip over to his workbench and marvel as he began to shape the ivory into handles to soon grace a prized revolver.

The first piece he worked on was none other than George Read's personnel .44 caliber Model 1860 Army Colt, cap and ball revolver. George had confidently allowed Duma the freedom of choosing the design, trusting in his artistic ability to select the right scene to carve. He was delighted when Duma began to form the head of a bull elephant on the piece of ivory in his special vise. Working long into the nights, it took Duma but a few days to craft and polish both handles and to fit them onto the revolver. As soon as it was finished, George Read was proudly running around the factory showing off his new revolver handle, making sure to point out the tiny cheetah paw print on the bottom of the handle. More importantly, he reminded everyone that Duma was now a major and permanent part of, what would soon be known the world over, as Pratt Read and Company.

At the end of the first work week Duma was called over to George Read's office. Mr. Read was smiling as he handed Duma a pay slip that read; *"Duma, wage value earned, $4.73."*

Duma, confused, looked up at the man's smiling face and simply asked, "What is this strange parchment?"

George Read threw back his head and roared with laughter. He had been expecting that Duma would be overjoyed with his first payment for the work he had done, but he had completely forgotten that Duma would have no idea what money was. He would have some teaching to do once they were home that evening. Duma was more than pleased as Mr. Read explained rudimentary finance to him. He not only felt joyful that he would now be able to pay for his own room and board each week, making him truly free and independent, but he also loved the "carvings" on the shiny bright coins that the paymaster had given him in return for his strange paper. *"Someday,"* he thought, *"I will carve a coin as well as these coins are carved."*

After Duma began to feel more comfortable in his new surroundings, he asked George Read if he could have a small piece of ivory in place of one week's pay for himself. George agreed; Duma was soon wearing a small ivory pendant around his neck in the shape of a coin. On it he had carefully carved a cheetah paw print next to what only could be a symbol of a mountain.

"This way, both Mlima and I can be together again," he said to himself.

By springtime, with the able assistance of George Read, who helped him manage his money, Duma, spent his spare time watching the shad fishermen haul in their catches, and was able to purchase an old wooden rowboat and some nets badly in need of mending. He began his new adventure of fishing the Connecticut River shad run. He quickly became adept at figuring the ins and outs of the shad business and turned his new found interest into a money producing venture. Once again, his love for hard work had returned to him, not only real value, but the dignity that had been stolen from him by the slavers.

One warm spring day, after Duma had just finished spreading his nets out to dry on some stacked boxes on the dock and was placing his catch of shad into crates for smoking, he heard his name being spoken. He looked up to see his friend and employer, George Read, and another man, rather well dressed for the docks sporting a carefully trimmed moustache and beard. He didn't quite hear the man's name when he was introduced by George, because he was too busy smiling and pumping the man's extended hand with his own, which was, unfortunately, a hand still covered with the foul smelling slime of fresh fish.

It didn't deter the man at all; whom Duma later learned was none other than the famous Sam Colt, who wanted to personally meet the man who would soon be carving handles for a matched set of his own special revolvers. It would be Duma's fine craftsmanship on Sam Colt's revolvers that would later on, help set off demand for them among European nobility.

CHAPTER TWELVE
El Baba meets Parliament

L IFE HAD ALSO changed over the last few years for Duma's brother "el Baba," as he now preferred to be called. His adventure began after leaving the Sultan's palace and a frustrated Majid behind forever. Learning a sufficient amount of the Queen's language along the way from Trevor Southerland, they sailed first to Bombay, and Ceylon, and eventually made their way to London and the House of Parliament, where el Baba's awaited testimony about the East African slave trade and its relationship to the ivory and spice industry would be a rather unique historical event.

One June day in 1873, El Baba, now dressed in good quality Indian cotton clothing and standing tall next to Lieutenant Southerland on the deck of a sleek British frigate, arrived at the mouth of the Thames River in London, prepared in his heart to tell first-hand, the story of the wretched inhumanity of the slave trade taking place in the Indian Ocean. He would soon have an opportunity to describe the interconnection between slavery, and the exotic spice and ivory trades birthed in Zanzibar, a protectorate of the British Crown.

In his most vivid imagination he could not have conceived of the shear advancements of mankind as he now stood in awe of nineteenth century London.

"*It is magic,*" he thought, as his gaze fell upon the approaching massive Westminster Palace with its famed Big Ben clock tower that stood taller than the tallest trees in el Baba's homeland. "This marvelous palace is finer than that of all the Sultan's palaces in the world together," he exclaimed, to Consul Southerland, who was not only his only connection to this new world, but the man to whom he would forever be indebted. This was the man who had obtained his freedom from Sayyid bin Majid; he was a man who was rapidly becoming el Baba's friend. The same Lieutenant Southerland, who now helped el Baba prepare for his new life in England, would serve as his official advisor for his talk to Parliament. This was a Parliament that was no longer a friend to slavery and now vigorously sought to remove all vestiges of it from their Empire.

The historic day when a simple slave from Tanganyika would address this body of leaders was finally upon them. Consul Southerland was eager to begin, but upon entering the famed Westminster Hall, the mighty el Baba felt small and humble, and he hesitated to continue after he looked around the massive room, and saw every man staring at him intensely.

Seated at a table in the center of the great House of Lords while Sutherland spoke first, el Baba was unable to concentrate on the proceedings because he had never been in so magnificent a building before. His appreciative eyes kept being drawn up high to the gilded ceilings and the large murals on the far wall. "*More riches than the entire wealth of Persia,*" he thought, marveling at the flamboyant show of ambiance in this House of Lords.

The angry chorus of voices brought his attention back quickly to the matter at hand. Parliament can be a fairly unruly place when passions get aroused and on the issue of slavery those passions had been aroused for some time now. They had recently been exacerbated by the recent writings of Henry M Stanley. As a result of his expedition into Tanganyika searching for the famed Dr. Livingston, Stanley had documented for Britain and the world the horrid situation of East African slaves. In addition, the United States had just finished fighting a war with its own people to end slavery a few years ago and other western nations had begun to move toward emancipation. To still have within its empire and under its protection the enslavement of Africans, was a serious discomfort to Britain. Having such lengthy and open defiance of the agreements she imposed upon the Sultans of Zanzibar, was the central source of irritation.

It seemed typical of politicians that, each person who questioned Lieutenant Southerland, chose to attack him personally for their own failure to stop the slave market in the Indian Ocean.

"How long will you continue to tolerate this unsavory condition?" he was asked accusingly, as if he alone caused, or could stop the countries of the world from purchasing slaves.

"We have gunships patrolling the shores and in the seas interdicting illegal slave dhows, regularly, your lordships. The slave markets on the Arabian Peninsula alone have kept us rather busy, I'm afraid," said a rapidly fatiguing Consul Southerland, "And then there's the oriental demand."

"Do we need to use force against the new Sultan of Zanzibar to get him to understand that we will no longer tolerate such a situation?" another Lord suggested, pressing the issue even further.

"Even if you should successfully do such a thing, you'll still not stop the selling of black flesh on the mainland from Kilwa to Mombasa, sir. Our fleet alone can't do it. Perhaps, some pressure placed by this Parliament on the purchasers?" his voice trailed off.

"If this new Sultan won't stop the trade, maybe we need to annex the entire island," said another, causing a flurry of babble that took a long time to settle in that room full of outspoken men.

El Baba, uneasy now, started to regret that he had ever come to London. He didn't understand every word, but he knew anger when he saw it, and, he watched as his good friend, Trevor Southerland began to falter under the constant barrage from the sanctimonious politicians in their fury. It was as if the entire business of selling flesh was Southerland's fault. They were ignoring the reality that the practice of slavery had also been heavily engaged in by the Crown herself in past years, certainly with the approval of this same House of Lords.

A drained Lieutenant Southerland, finished with his last round of questioning, turned toward el Baba, motioning for him to rise, that he might speak to the chagrined nobility.

More intimidating than the angry assaults, was the absolute silence that greeted el Baba. Each member glared intensely at this humble giant of a man. Gathering his dignity, he stood with Duma's ivory cane in his tightly gripped hand, and prepared to tell them of his personal experiences with the East African slave trade.

El Baba began his story speaking in slow deliberate English. He told of the African tribal chiefs that gained great power and wealth by capturing slaves and destroying their villages and how they then turned them over to the Omani slave traders. He spoke at length about the hardships and the disease faced by the long ivory caravans; the chains, the whips, the guns, the paucity of food and drink. He made many points about the Arab porter's casual concern for the well being of the slaves, and how easily replacements could be obtained, should any slave falter on the centuries old caravan routes leading from the far interior to Bagamoya and Zanzibar. He spoke of the open slave market in Stone Town, and how lately, slaves were being hid in caves, and put on dhows in the dark of night to avoid British detection. He told of the many times he had heard his previous master, Sultan

Majid, make light of the treaties, and of his insincere promises to cut down on the slave trade. He explained that the need for slaves was driven by the world's insatiable hunger for ivory and spices. And then, he told the story of his family; his parents and sister's death, his brother's unknown fate; he finished with his own story of being forced to become the Sultan's personal body guard.

When he ended, there was a long pause of silence as each and every pair of eyes in that magnificent hall bore into his soul. He couldn't decide whether this great sea of expressionless faces reminded him of a pack of well fed lions who had just finished their feast, or a pride of the predatory beasts about to pounce on their newest selected victim.

The applause, which began slowly at first from someone in the back of the crowd of faces, spread rhythmically, not unlike the drums from his village in Tanganyika. At its peak it was all consuming, like the sounds of the great waterfalls of Africa. Finally, each member rose to their feet; some whistling, while still others began enthusiastically stamping their feet.

One had to wonder if they were applauding el Baba or their own good sense in attempting to stop the horrors of the slave trade they had previously engaged in themselves; enslaving millions of Western Africans for Jamaica and their Caribbean colonies. Was not at least part of this crescendo merely an attempt by parliament to rid itself of its own guilt? Yes, it was true that they now tried to abolish, not only the slave trade, but slavery itself. However, that trade still continued, unabated, in their protectorates in Zanzibar and the Indian Ocean. This was both a source of great discomfort and severe political pressure for each of them.

The unique event of el Baba's reception was stunning, and one that was to determine el Baba's new direction in life. London was alive for weeks with chatter of el Baba's address to the House of Lords. Nearly every person, from every walk of life, learned of the tall African ex-slave named, el Baba. The nation had reached the point of no return now, and there would be no turning its back on its efforts to wipe out the last vestiges of slavery in its empire. El Baba had now become a symbol of that effort and would soon begin his new role as official ambassador of that cause.

The days and months ahead were a whirlwind of activity for el Baba; he entered the world of British nobility as if he were the latest fashion trend. Permanently assigned to be at his side was none other than Trevor Sutherland, who was relieved to be out from under the constant pressure from Parliament, and thrust into, what few minor officers ever experience, a life among the upper class.

To Southerland's credit, he refrained from encouraging el Baba to become a mere novelty to be passed around among the well-off. There was a mission to accomplish and the message needed to move beyond the constant ceremony and the grand party stage if it were to be effective. Trevor also well understood that he needed to win over this aristocracy, if he were to succeed. So he began to shape el Baba into what they expected. First and foremost, he dressed him in the fine traditional clothing of the wealthiest of African tribal chiefs. It mattered not that he had been but a common village man; he now was out to impress as many as he could with the urgency of his mission.

El Baba understood what was happening very well. Had he not watched these same games played by the many visitors to the Sultan? When stalking game, back in Tanganyika, he learned that the hunter must blend into the surroundings in order to complete his mission, and so now, he too must do the same by wearing fine robes, learning to smile, and to speak the tongue of the very people who could help stop the slavery of his people. He was marvelously equipped for the role; his deep voice, massive body, and friendly smile easily captured the hearts of the British with ease.

Another aspect of British abolitionist sentiment had also

been a key element in the years leading up to the American War Between the States. And, that was that the British Colony of Canada, under Queen Victoria, had strongly encouraged slaves, escaping from the South of the United States, by way of the Underground Railroad, to settle safely in Canada. Much appreciation was given to Queen Victoria, for her sympathy to the plight of the slave. However, it was still the greatest of surprises when a royal courier arrived with a sealed letter at the quarters of Lieutenant Trevor Southerland. It was from Queen Victoria, requesting an audience with el Baba. The Queen had apparently heard of el Baba's reputation and his mission, and she decided to place her personal "*imprimatur*" upon it.

El Baba hadn't, until now, comprehended his importance to British society, but he knew that it was extremely rare that a lowly villager and ex-slave from interior Africa would be honored with an invitation to go before the Queen of England. Trevor Southerland, in his excitement, had thrust the letter with the Queen's seal into the large hands of el Baba and said, "My God, it's the Queen, el Baba, and she wants to meet us … you …. Read it yourself." He was forgetting completely that reading English wasn't yet one of el Baba's skills, though he had learned a lot of the spoken language over the last few years by listening to British dignitaries, and talking with Trevor Sutherland almost daily, since he left Zanzibar.

"What does it say?" el Baba asked, though he had heard clearly what the Lieutenant had just said. "Are we going to the palace my good friend?"

His large hands, the hands of a warrior strong enough to guard a Sultan, began to tremble slightly as he thought about what once seemed impossible.

"Perhaps, she can find Duma for me?"

"Oh, my dear friend, I'm afraid she can't. I mean that we can't ask the Queen for such a favor. I'm certain we wouldn't be able to find him, el Baba."

"He is in America, is he not?" asked el Baba, showing that he simply didn't understand just how large America was.

Aware that el Baba had been devoted to his younger brother, and often spent much of his time cherishing Duma's ivory cane, he wisely gave him little encouragement.

"Perhaps someday, my friend, maybe you will go to America to search for Duma, but, for now, we must just talk about stopping the slavery."

CHAPTER THIRTEEN
But he must wear a sword

"WHAT ARE THESE regulations you speak of my good friend?" asked el Baba.

"It is the Lord Chamberlain's traditional dress requirements for all those who would go before the Queen in Buckingham Palace, el Baba. The rules, I'm afraid, are quite rigid."

"But, my good friend, I am not a British subject, as much as that is an honor, I am a free African, am I not?"

"But the Queen is the Queen, is she not?" replied Trevor Southerland, now aroused with fear that el Baba would not comply with the necessary British rules of nobility.

"I would not be so bold as to tell the Queen what to wear, if she were to visit me in my village. This clothing I wear represents my home, Lieutenant. And I shall wear it or nothing at all."

"My dear, el Baba, I don't know what to tell you," said a very concerned young officer, whose dream of going before the Queen was being shattered before his very eyes. Yet, he had to admit that the sight of this tall muscular African in the required silk velvet waistcoat, wig and white stockings with gold trimmed embroidered lace on his collar and cuffs, wouldn't really do dignity to his stature either.

"I will contact the queen's courier el Baba, to find if an exception can be made for you, but I have little hope for that to occur as such a thing is unheard of."

Inwardly, Trevor Southerland admired this man greatly. He had personally seen him risk his life to stand up to the Sultan Majid and now he is again sufficiently proud to totally disregard the proper protocol required to be in the presence of Queen Victoria.

It only took one day for Buckingham Palace to reply. Again, Trevor Southerland's hands trembled. He broke the seal on the letter, as if it might somehow contain the announcement of his own execution ordered by the queen herself. His eyes grasped the message instantly; it contained but one line, and in the personal handwriting of the Queen, no less, *"But, of course, he must wear a sword!"*

Instant relief overcame the anxious lieutenant, as he announced the contents to el Baba. "You may wear your ceremonial tribal clothing, but you must also wear a ceremonial sword, el Baba."

"Do tribal chiefs wear swords?" responded el Baba promptly.

Lieutenant Southerland thought quickly, "Those who are also powerful warriors do."

El Baba hesitated, and then looked at his good friend, and sensing his anxiety over the issue, he said, "Then I shall wear a sword also."

It wasn't difficult to determine which of the two men was more enchanted with the visit to Buckingham Palace and the Queen. It was Lieutenant Trevor Sutherland. Dressed in his finest military uniform complete with gold braids, buttons and the ceremonial sword, he was a dashing figure, but once there, he was more like a giddy child in a new playroom. Just looking at the ostentatious palace, with its ornate gates, its gardens, and massive façade, caused him to falter a bit in his step, not at all maintaining the carriage of the dignified officer that he was. Once el Baba and he were inside the palace, it was more difficult for him to maintain his composure. As the two men were escorted up the famed grand staircase, he broke with all attempts to appear in control, and allowed himself to spin and turn in every direction. He was in absolute awe of the shear elegance, everywhere.

El Baba, couldn't believe how anyone, be they tribal chief, Sultan, wealthy merchant, or even a Queen, could possibly have amassed enough wealth in a lifetime to command ownership of even one small room, out of the hundreds that this fine palace possessed.

They were escorted into a waiting area outside the White Drawing Room where Queen Victoria was already engaged in conducting an audience with some sort of minor dignitary. After being directed to a flamboyantly upholstered bench, one of the Queen's aides quietly informed them of the proper comportment expected of one when meeting the Queen. This caused Trevor Southerland to become even more certain that he was actually living in a dream.

Seated in a chair next to them was a well dressed gentleman that appeared not to be intimidated by the whole affair at all. Perhaps, because he wasn't a British subject, but an American with a mission to eventually sell his fine guns to the British military, after properly softening up the decision, first, by offering a gift of beautiful, matched ivory-handled, .44 cal., Colt pistols to the Queen. In minutes, they were chatting, and Sam Colt, always looking for someone to hear of his fine guns, offered to show them the pistols he had fashioned for the Queen.

"These are the finest revolvers made," he assured the two men, "and the finest ivory carving in the world."

El Baba's attention was instantly captured as he studied the elegant gold-inlaid and ornately engraved pistols nestled in the velvet case on Sam Colt's lap. His heart thought of Duma as he searched the handle design for evidence that the carving was not as good as Duma could do. The regal horses on the handles were indeed fine carving, he thought, but he was also certain that Duma could do as well were he offered the opportunity.

Trevor was quite appreciative of the weaponry and asked the gentleman his name; hoping that someday he might be in a position of sufficient wealth to make such a purchase himself.

"Sam Colt, from Hartford, Hartford, Connecticut," he amended, worried that these British might dare to confuse it with Hertford England, just east of London.

Just as Sam offered to let the officer handle one of the ornate pistols, an aide announced that el Baba and Lieutenant Southerland should, "Please step forward to the entrance of the White Drawing Room. The Queen is prepared to greet you gentlemen now."

Another quirk of life is that we are so unaware of those occasions of fate that sneak ever so close to our consciousness, but for the slightest of reasons, we miss great opportunity by mere inches or seconds. Little did el Baba suspect that the ivory handles he had just admired were carved by his brother, Duma. Had a moment more passed, the pistols would have been taken out of their custom shaped beds in the velvet case for Trevor to handle, and he would have then noticed the tell-tale symbol of the tiny cheetah paw neatly hidden on the bottom of the ivory handles. It would then have been but one or two simple questions which would have provided el Baba with an easy path to his brother, Duma, a brother he would never in his life see again.

But, completely enthralled with the wondrous vision before his eyes, the unsuspecting el Baba moved on. The White Drawing Room was a spectacle of gold and white, from gold-tasseled draperies to chandeliers, over a dozen in that one room. It was difficult to take it all in: the scalloped gold braids on the upper room walls, the overly ornate frames on both mirrors and paintings, the fresh floral arrangements hovering over rich exotic veneered tables, the plush upholstered benches and chairs hosting gold trimmed pillows, and a rug, more grand than imaginable, lining the entire room.

It was at that moment that an overwhelmed Lieutenant Southerland, allowing himself to forget his proper court manners, inadvertently emitted an audible whistle, causing the queen who had been busy at the desk by a window, to pause from her work and look up.

"Gentlemen," she approached them, "it is I who am honored to meet you," she said, thrusting her hand toward el Baba. "You are the talk of the Parliament and London's many garden parties, and I'm delighted to personally welcome you to London, el Baba."

The usual niceties disposed of, Queen Victoria, dressed in royal finery customary for holding audiences, began to discuss the reason that she had chosen to summon the two to Buckingham Palace.

"It is this abominable slavery thing," she told them. "For years now, we have been trying to pursue its elimination throughout the Empire, with treaties and gunships, but as you both know, it is a difficult thing to eliminate entirely such a lucrative enterprise. I would like to try still another approach, have you act as my personal emissary to both Europe and the rest of the Empire as well. I would hope that you, being an ex-slave, would be able to add your personal knowledge and conviction to the British message that slavery will no longer be tolerated, and that we seek other nation's cooperation in terminating this horrible business. The slavers and the slave buyers need to learn that I'm not playing pat a cake with them anymore."

"How am I, but an ex-slave, to be powerful enough to be able to tell such important leaders what to do, your majesty?" asked el Baba in all sincerity.

"You'll be speaking for me, personally, el Baba. I will give you this Letter of Credence to introduce yourself on my behalf, to both, political leaders and nobility. I will award you some sort of honorary title to impress them with, and you will draw from the treasury sufficient funds to complete your mission properly. Do you agree to undertake such a task, el Baba?"

"I will be honored to do this work for both of us," el Baba said, with a smile of confidence in what he had just agreed to do. He did have one other concern though.

"I'm afraid, your majesty, that I wouldn't quite know the proper way of accomplishing this mission without my friend, Lieutenant Sutherland here…"

"I have arranged to assign Commander Southerland to be both your aide and to act as your official advisor. As your Marshall, he will show you what is needed, and how to accomplish it."

Trevor Southerland began to feel his heart race. "*The Queen has made a horrible mistake. I am but a mere lieutenant, can she not see by the markings on my uniform? What am I to do, for one simply does not correct the Queen?*"

"Your Majesty?"

"You'll find your new quarters at the London Embassy, Commander, and your new uniforms. We can't have a mere lieutenant representing the Crown, can we?" she said resolutely, and then she smiled.

"Thank you, your Majesty; I shall do my best to….."

"I know you will, both of you. I would suggest that you start with the French and the Germans, both who could benefit from a little prodding. Don't you agree?"

"Yes, your Majesty."

"I do so wish it were possible to stop people from assisting the purchasing of slaves from Africa, she offered."

El Baba, always a man of truth and great character responded, though quite inappropriately to a queen. "There is enough gold right here in this one room to buy the freedom of all the slaves in Africa, your Majesty."

Ignoring el Baba's embarrassing observation, Queen Victoria looked at her aide standing nearby and signaled the audience was over. He waited just briefly for the usual formalities to conclude, and then led the pair out of the magnificent room.

Once again, as they were leaving, el Baba passed within inches of his brother Duma's hidden cheetah print. He merely nodded at Sam Colt as he entered to present his matched pistols to the Queen.

Trevor was the first to speak as the coach pulled away from the palace.

"Well good friend, it looks as if we're both going to enter a different life from now on."

"Yes my friend, Lieutenant Trevor. I am greatly glad that you will be staying with me on this new journey."

"I am too, el Baba, I am too, but there is one thing?"

"Yes?"

"It's Commander now?"

They both laughed and el Baba said, "May I keep the sword, Commander?"

"Keep whatever you wish my good friend; we are doing the Queen's labor with the use of her treasury."

"El Baba?"

"Yes Trevor?"

"Did you really mean to tell the Queen that she could purchase all the slaves in Africa, if she wanted to? I couldn't believe my ears."

"Trevor?"

"Yes, Mr. Emissary?"

"Is it your Lord Chamberlain's protocol that allowed you to whistle at the Queen?"

The laughter from the two continued all the way to the Embassy.

CHAPTER FOURTEEN
Years later, back to Zanzibar

THERE IS MORE irony in life sometimes than one could deliberately plan. El Baba's storied life was no exception. He had met a wonderful lady at the French court in Paris and charmed her sufficiently to broach the subject of marriage. It became a marriage which eventually produced several well-disciplined children who, unlike their father, had all the advantages of being raised with the finer things that a diplomat's life afforded.

A mature Captain Southerland and an older el Baba had been well accepted across the Empire by those who supported their cause, though several in the Empire, particularly those in the protectorates, continued to resist the complete termination of the slave trade, at least whenever they could get away with it. Little by little the reluctant were reduced to complying with the demands of the British Empire that always treated the reality of the situation in as practical a manner as possible. They simply forced the protectorates to follow their rules by installing them into treaties and trade agreements. Just to make certain, there was always the persuasion of compliance in the form of the

Imperial navy and marines. Nothing served the Empire better, in terms of backing up their requests, than the power of their ships' cannons.

It was irony that brought both el Baba and Trevor back to Zanzibar where they first had met. Once the hub and center of open slavery, Zanzibar had gradually been forced to reduce much of the open trade in human flesh under its sovereignty by a continued series of agreements imposed upon them by the United Kingdom. One such agreement with the Crown required that prior approval be obtained before any change in Sultans occurred. It just so happened that this agreement was egregiously violated at the very time el Baba and Captain Southerland were visiting as the Crown's emissaries.

The death of Sultan Hamad ibn Thuwaini occurred suddenly and a power grab of the Sultanate itself was made by Khalid, who took the liberty of installing himself as the new Sultan of Zanzibar in direct defiance of the treaty. The British Empire didn't achieve its power and size by allowing lesser powers to defy them, nor could it afford to allow such disobedience, by weaker entities.

El Baba and Trevor Sutherland were conveniently available to act as emissaries on behalf of the Crown. Khalid would have little respect for the British and even less for their treaty. He allowed an audience with the two men primarily to assert his newly felt authority.

"This is certainly a bigger and more prestigious palace since we last were in Zanzibar my good friend el Baba. Let us hope our past success in outsmarting our adventurous Sultan, Majid, is soon repeated again with this Khalid." Trevor, who intended to impress the renegade sultan, was in full dress uniform,.

"My Captain, if those war vessels with their armament pointed at this palace don't bring fear to his heart, I wonder what chance there is that he will back down," said el Baba.

"Remember, that we are not the military commanders, but

emissaries of Queen Victoria, who prefers that we settle this conflict without fighting, if possible."

"We shall see my friend; if this is to be accomplished."

The men were escorted into the Sultan's chamber where the defiant Khalid was seated; he was surrounded by a dozen or so armed guards, and two traditional guards with ornate scimitars, prepared to be used, if necessary.

"Ah," said Khalid, "we have an officer and a slave here to speak for the Queen. Is she too weak to speak for herself?"

El Baba, ignored the rude affront to both the queen and him, made as gracious a bow before the Sultan as he could, and thus, effectively counteracted Sayyid Khalid's insults with courtesy.

"My good Khalid, it is most enlightening to see you sitting in the Sultan's seat, but I'm afraid that it is a seat ill gotten according to your predecessor's word in our treaty," said el Baba.

"Your reputation for diplomacy precedes you el Baba, but it is of little value in Zanzibar. The Queen of England may hold preference for you, but I, the new Sultan of Zanzibar, simply do not. Be quick! What is it you've come to say?"

"We've come to remind you of your treaty obligations, Khalid," said the officer. "It is not the queen's desire to use force; but if your sultanate seeks to be valid, it must be approved by her first."

"Strange, isn't it, I don't recall signing any treaty, Captain," said the Sultan, reaching for a piece of fruit to accent his lack of concern about the military tension that was building rapidly on the island.

"I have a message here from the Rear-Admiral Ralston, commander of the Crown's naval forces out in the harbor. I would advise you to think over his directives carefully."

One of the Sultan's guards stepped forward; took the sealed paper from Captain Southerland, and brought it to Khalid who opened it up.

"An ultimatum? This man believes that he is in a position to give me an ultimatum? I am Sultan of Zanzibar now and when his deadline of nine in the morning arrives, I will still be Zanzibar's proud Sultan. Don't you realize that I, Khalid, have more than enough brave soldiers and navy to cast your fleet to the bottom of the sea?" he shouted, throwing the parchments angrily in the direction of el Baba and Trevor.

Ignoring the threat, Trevor Southerland retorted, "You have but a few thousand men and just one small pleasure craft against five modern military vessels fitted with the latest armament. I'm afraid you'll be destroyed rather quickly if you persist in pretending to be the Sultan after the time allotted you is up."

"See them out, guards. You're both lucky I don't send your wretched, quartered and drawn carcasses out to the commander for his dinner!"

Having failed in their mission to convince this fool of a man that he was about to die, Trevor and el Baba both gave a gracious bow before turning and retreating.

The boat ride back to the HMS St.George was a short one. Within minutes, they were relating what had occurred to Rear-Admiral Ralston, who was commander of the British fleet.

"Sir, I'm afraid that the man refuses to move," said Captain Trevor.

"Then we shall move him, ourselves, in the morning, Captain."

Admiral Ralston then turned to his junior officer and quietly gave the necessary commands.

"Prepare for battle, secure all ships, and align all armament on the castle. Intercept any and all craft, small or large, in the harbor not belonging to the Crown and if they resist, sink them."

El Baba had seen men die before, but he had never been in a war. He could not believe that diplomacy had failed. This pretend sultan, Khalid, was about to feel the wrath of the entire British Empire, and those puny stone walls of his palace wouldn't help him one bit.

"Why is it men, because of their thirst for power and wealth,

make such foolish choices, bringing great harm to themselves?" he wondered.

The sun rose brightly that next morning, and surprisingly little activity occurred that was visible. As usual in Zanzibar, the gulls greeted the day by floating elegantly over the harbor, searching for a meal, hardly expecting the disruption that would occur. The slight breeze brought the usual aroma of cloves and cinnamon from nearby, Pemba, to permeate the air while hardly a military person was visible. It appeared, a day like any other.

All strategic positions in preparation for battle by both adversaries had been taken the night before. As the time approached, the admiral summoned the two diplomats.

"For your own safety, you gentlemen had better stay below," said the Commander. There is no need any longer for diplomacy. It shall be our ship's cannons that will enforce this treaty in a moment or two."

The bombardment from the cannons and the machine gun fire began shortly after nine in the morning as promised. Round after round tore into the palace walls tearing huge chunks of stone and mortar and reducing much of it to rubble. Fire broke out and the man who would be Sultan was forced to flee. There were a few final, less dramatic skirmishes among the troops on land and other ships at sea, which culminated in the sinking of the one wooden ship Khalid had for his forces. In little more than half of an hour the war was over, and not one British man was killed, while many hundreds of Khalid's troops were slaughtered.

The history books would record the battle between the British Empire and the Sultan of Zanzibar, as the shortest of wars, ever.

El Baba had but one word to say as he and Trevor Southerland watched the Sultan's shattered flag being removed from the crumbled palace, "Suicide!"

CHAPTER FIFTEEN
My God, it worked!

I T HAD ACTUALLY happened. Just moments before, the three young students had been standing in the Gothart Collection room of the old McClelland Library on Boston's North Street, touching an old worn picture, and now, in an instant; they were back in time, as if they were right in the picture in the middle of the dirt covered, main street and looking up at a sign on the large factory building that read; Pratt, Read and Co. Deep River, Connecticut.

Jason, somehow wearing the appropriate clothing of the time, was the first to speak.

"My God, it worked!" he exclaimed.

"You'll get used to it, after awhile Jason," said Sam with her usual smile. "Shall we be going inside?"

"Here we go again," quipped Jonah, "off to the salt mines."

"He just detests doing any hard work, Jason. Pay him little attention."

Sam started walking toward the wooden structure.

"Stop, we can't go in there asking for jobs!" Jason said, with some alarm to his voice.

"Why not?" asked Jonah.

"Because, we're too young. You Americans must have child labor laws?"

Sam threw her head back and laughed. "I fear Jason that you don't yet understand. This is 1881, now. There are no child labor laws; just about everyone works, and …"

Jonah spoke, "We've got to get inside to really learn what happens to the ivory once it reaches Connecticut, and we'll have to find a place to stay too."

It was certainly an interesting picture when the door of the Pratt, Read factory opened up. Three young people, a young white lad, a tall black youngster and a disheveled girl, were standing there adorned in somewhat, less than new clothes; each one holding an old canvas traveling bag stuffed with their clothing. They had, so they told it, just arrived in town from Boston, to find work in the ivory mills.

The ivory business was in its heyday during the new industrial age, and non-skilled labor was always in demand. Though skilled labor was being imported, there was always room for a few common working hands to help out for a while.

"We're just hiring for a while, no more than a month, folks. The hours are long and the work is dirty. Do you have a place to stay?" muttered Silas Hubbard the accountant hardly looking up from his books.

"No sir, we'll need to find a place," said Jonah.

"You'll need to go see old Billy Winters up the street at his livery. He'll get you a place to stay either in town or over at Comstock's in Ivoryton, a few miles walk." Then, without missing a breath he added, "Pay's a dollar fifty cents a day for ten hours honest work. If you work helping Billy in his livery with the mules and wagons there's an extra fifty cents a week in it for you. Do you want the job?"

The three looked at each other, each of them aware that they couldn't earn even one week's allowance in months at these low pay rates, and then they nodded yes.

"Good. Young lady, you report to Sam Waterfield across the street in the number one bleach house. Leave your bag under those coats hanging on the back wall for now. What's your name, for my pay books?"

"Sam, sir."

"Are you a boy?"

"No sir, it's short for Samantha."

"Then you'll be Samantha. We don't need any confusion around here. We got enough Sams working already, and they're all rightfully boys."

"Young fella?"

Jonah stepped forward and asked, "Yes?"

"Not you son, I meant the Negro lad."

Jason, hesitating, uncomfortable with being called that name for the first time in his life, swallowed hard and said, "Yes sir," not letting on that he already had many times the education of this somewhat brusque man. There would be some things he would have to get use to with this time travel business.

"You'll be working up at the livery for Billy Winters, but he won't tolerate much laying around. He expects each penny paid to be earned. Do you understand?"

"Yes sir."

"Okay. Go up and meet him, and learn the layout, and what's expected of you. You'll all start in the morning 6:30 sharp. If you're late, you're out of a job, understand?"

"You young fella," he said, looking at Jonah.

"Sir?"

"You'll work here in the shop doing odd jobs, whatever is needed; cleaning, errands, and such. See me at 6:30 sharp."

"Thank you, sir."

No one paid attention to the black man in the front workbench, carving an antlered buck's head on a small piece of ivory. He certainly noticed the three new workers, especially

Jason. He hadn't seen any new Negroes around Deep River since Billy Winters brought up his gang of relatives from down South some years ago.

"I'll be meeting him soon," he thought to himself. *"Maybe I can teach him some ivory carving tricks?"*

Billy Winters was hammering a new wheel on a cart with a ten pound sledge when Jason showed up in the doorway.

"What can I do for you young man?" asked the bearded man who had, thanks to the help of George Read, become quite prosperous since first coming, some years back, to Deep River as a runaway slave.

"Fella down at the Pratt Read factory told me to report for work here. He said we'd be starting in the morning, and that you'd help us find a place to sleep nights."

"Whacha mean, 'us?'"

"I have two friends," he hesitated for a second, and then he added, "A couple of white kids, a girl and a boy."

Winters looked into this youngster's eyes. He had long ago learned how the world ran and it wasn't often that white kids, even fifteen years after the Civil War, were that friendly with Negroes.

"I got a place for you here in town with me, but your friends might want to use a place I know in Iv'ryton, lot's of white folks there...."

"My name is Jason and we'll stay together, Sir."

"Are you sure, Son?"

"If you got room for all three of us, I'm sure."

Billy shrugged without comment and casually responded, "Y'all have to ride home in the back of my wagon, Jason. Where are y'all from? You got a strange sound in your words and it sure ain't from the South."

"Boston, sir. We're all from Boston."

"Well Jason, you sounds like theys teach you pretty good up there, but what we needs here is some muscle and a strong back, so's all that book learnin won't help you much."

"I can handle the work, Mr. Winters. I have an exercise plan I follow."

"What's that, Son?"

Jason caught himself speaking as if he were still back in Boston. *"I have to be more careful,* he thought."

"I'm plenty strong enough, Mr. Winters."

"You'll need it, Jason. You'll need it."

Jason thanked him and as he turned to leave, Billy Winters lit a cigar and said to himself, *"there's something strange about that boy."*

The wagon ride that evening was more fun than they had imagined; as the trio of visitors bounced and tumbled around laughing as the wagon slowly headed out to the edge of town. Billy Winters had managed to purchase a large home once his business started doing well and his kinfolks all built houses on his property at the north end of town. They were heading there to their new home for a while.

"You kids got some food?"

"No sir," answered Sam.

"How you gonna work if y'all don't eat?" he asked, knowing the answer already.

"It'll cost you fifty cents a day each for room and board. Can't afford to feed everyone old Silas Hubbard hires for free, can I?" he fibbed.

Billy would do anything for George Read's Company, he was, after all the man who risked jail and the loss of his business, to hide him for those years leading up to the Civil War.

"Jus so ya know," he warned them, "in my house, we all wash up and give thanks, before we eats the Lord's food."

Jason LeBlanc smiled just a bit, as he realized, right then, that there was little difference between this simple man and his well educated father. *"Maybe most fathers,"* he decided privately, *"are the same inside."*

It was a few hours later, after the dishes were washed and properly put away, when Billy Winters' idea of fatherhood became evident. Gathering his two youngsters, Freda and Benjamin, up in his arms on the couch, he started telling them a story about how, "A long time ago, two mules, a dark mule and a light-colored mule, was goin along a narrow mount'n trail in different directions, each refusing to move for the other, each believin they was the most important, and so neither mule would move."

"What happened, Daddy?" asked Freda, who was eager to know the outcome.

"I'll bet that light-colored mule wins," said her older brother Ben, cynically, "cause them dark-coloreds always lose."

Jonah glanced at Sam curled up on the floor, then he glanced at Jason to see if he had a reaction. Jason, sensing correctly that Billy Winters had a message for all of them with his story telling, just winked back at Jonah.

"Well if you go up that mountain today," Billy continued, "When you gets to that place where them two mules met; you will see nuthin much but an old pile of bones, cept maybe a vulture or two still pickin on the last of them carcasses."

"Eeeeww!" cried Freda, "That's not a nice story, Daddy."

"Why not Freda?" asked her father.

"Cause the ending is nasty and mean for everybody."

"Un huh," said Billy, smiling broadly, "Tha's the idea, Honey. When people acts like stubborn old mules, they alls gets hurt badly."

"What would you do Jason, if you'd be that dark mule?" asked Ben, not yet happy with the outcome.

Every eye turned toward the young black man.

"How is he going to handle this one?" wondered Sam.

"Jason looked over at Benjamin, and responded, with a hint of a sparkle in his eyes, "Oh, that's easy Ben. I'd invite that old light-colored mule home for dinner and fill him up with buckets of good food until he forgot all about wanting to be stubborn."

Even Benjamin laughed at that answer, and so did everyone there, until Freda asked innocently enough, "Jus like Daddy did tonight with Jonah and Sam?"

The room grew uncomfortably silent, and Mrs. Winters looked at Billy, waiting for the proper answer that she knew he would give.

"Uh huh honey, that's jus what happened, cept these here two light-colored mules?"

"Yeah, Daddy?"

"Well, they wasn't stubborn, Honey. Theys moved first an asked me to take them home and feed them, so I's did. Don't see no vultures pickin anybody's bones around here, do you?" he asked, tickling her bare toes.

Before Freda could recover from giggling enough to respond, there was a soft, but distinct knock on the door. Mrs. Winters shushed the children down and opened the door. Standing there with a smile and a large package of smoked shad in his hand was Duma.

CHAPTER SIXTEEN
I have your cane

"THOUGHT IT TIME we'd meet, folks," said Duma with a shy smile.

"Well do come in son. Not too often I sees you without your carving tools or fishin nets," said Billy Winters rising off the couch to greet the younger man, who for many years now, hardly ever said much more than a "good morning" to him, as if they both being the same color was wrong.

"I've been meaning to meet you and your family since I first saw you in town, Mr. Winters."

"Well son, tha's been a while comin now, ain't it?"

"Yes sir, I guess I just didn't want to get too friendly," then, glancing at Billy's white visitors, Jonah and Samantha, added, "with my own kind."

Billy understood his motives and he decided to find more about this talented young man.

"Theys say at the factory that you the best at carvin them elephant teeth son," he said, leading Duma over to the kitchen table. "There's some beans left. Did you eat yet?"

"Yes sir, Mrs. Read, she cooks a fine meal, you know," said

Duma.

"Where'd you learn to carve ivory like that Son?"

"My name's Duma. It means, Cheetah, in Swahili."

"Don't know any Swahili, Duma," said Billy Winters.

Then he returned to the question he had yet to get an answer for. "Folks say that you have to know a lot to make ivory do what you want with a knife."

"I started to learn how to carve ivory as a young boy in my village, Sir. I taught myself with old ivory pieces lying around."

"So, you is from Africa, not the South?"

Duma, proudly answered him, "Tanganyika, Mr. Winters. Where are you from?"

"Where's Tanganyika, Duma?"

"I don't really know, except you can reach Zanzibar by walking toward the morning sun, many, many, days away from my village."

"It's on the Southeast coast of Africa, Duma," said Jason, "directly south of Kenya." He was tempted to tell him that Tanganyika had long since changed its name to Tanzania.

Both Billy and Duma looked at Jason, surprised that such a young Negro lad could know so much.

"I'm Jason, and these are my friends, Samantha and Jonah, Duma. We're from Boston."

They shook hands and Billy then told Duma everyone's name. He picked up Freda and gave her a big kiss which made her pucker up, and shrug her shoulders, causing everyone to laugh.

"What part of Africa are you from, Mr. Winters?" asked Duma.

"I was born on a plantation in South Carolina, Duma," he then added, with a bit of a twinkle in his eyes, "It's kinda far away from that Tang a…."

"Tanganyika, Sir."

Freda started singing a song as Billy put her down on the floor.

"Tan go yi ka, Tan go yi ka; bite my toe; bite my toe."

"It's time for the kids to go to bed," Billy announced, as he reached up on the shelf for his tin can, and a cigar."

All three of Mr. Macready's students realized they were already getting a better education about slavery than they ever could get in class.

"Would you like a good Connecticut cigar, Duma?"

"No thanks, Billy."

Duma was now comfortable enough to call him by his first name as practically everyone else in town did.

"I heard that you were an escaped slave, Billy," Duma commented.

"Yup, cept we was called runaways."

Again, glancing nervously at the two white kids, Duma continued, "Did you get whipped much?"

"Not much. I was a hard worker, one of the owner's best."

"Then, why'd you run away?"

"I heerd we was for sale, agin," said Billy, looking up at a cobweb on the ceiling, and blowing a puff of cigar smoke at it.

"How come you know so much about readin an talkin so fine, if you was a slave?" he asked Duma.

Duma decided it was alright for Billy to know how he learned to read. Maybe he knew anyway?

"Mrs. Cheney, she taught me in Zanzibar."

"Comstock Cheney, in Ivoryton, that Mrs. Cheney?"

"Uh huh, Sarah Cheney, the ivory buyer's wife."

"You was her slave?"

"She freed me and brought me over here...with my carving tools."

Sam, Jonah and Jason now moved over to the kitchen table and were taking mental notes as best they could. The conversation between these two very different ex-slaves became deeper as the evening passed on into night.

"How'd they catch you if you was a cheetah?"

"Other tribes caught me and turned me over to the Arab slave traders for a reward."

"Things in your village sounds same'd they was in America, a few years back, with us runaways, Duma. I hardly slept cause I fear'd them slave catchers takin me back."

"They burned my village and killed my mother and father. The ivory men; they shot my sister, just because she was sick."

"What ivory men?"

"Arabs, they used us for carrying ivory for months. When we got to Zanzibar, we and the ivory we carried was sold."

"You carried ivory?"

"My brother carried one end of a tusk, and I carried the other for months."

"What happened to your brother?"

"He was taken by the Sultan."

"Why you carve ivory when you know that it is only on the broken backs of black people that it is brought here?" Billy asked Duma.

"The ivory I carve is not the carvings of a slave; it is the carvings of a free black man; black man's art for all the world to see. It is not the ivory that is evil, but the men who deal in slavery. Now, I might ask you the same question. How can you smoke tobacco and wear cotton when you know it is because it is only on the broken backs of black people that it is here?"

Billy didn't answer. Maybe there wasn't an answer just yet.

"So you lost your freedom because of the ivory caravans?" said Billy stating an obvious fact, he never expected the answer Duma gave.

"I gained my freedom because of the ivory caravan."

After pausing and regaining his composure, Billy continued, "You mean because Mrs. Cheney gave you your freedom, don' cha?"

"No, I learned what freedom really meant, and I learned it while carrying the weight of that ivory tusk on my shoulder for hundreds of miles."

He then began to tell them about his vow to refuse to be a slave even if the traders owned his body. He told of surviving, only because he memorized for his art everything he saw, and how that kept his spirits up. They all were spellbound as he described the night when he was laying by the fire tired and hungry, watching a serpent moving freely through the banyan tree's branches, and how it meant freedom to him, and he told of how in his dream; he became a free serpent.

It was impossible to hide the tears sliding down his cheeks as he talked. Even Billy Winters wiped his own eyes a time or two during Duma's tale.

"Since then," he continued, "I will always be free, and so will my brother, Mlima, because I have captured our freedom in the ivory."

No one spoke for a moment until finally, Billy's wife, Lucretia, could stand it no longer and blurted out, "How'd you do that?"

Duma told of carving the serpents, one representing him and one for Mlima, which caused Jason to sit immediately erect.

"What kind of thing was this carving on?" he asked abruptly.

"It is on a cane, a fine cane," Duma said.

"Where is this cane now?" Jason pressed on, insisting, loudly enough to surprise everyone.

"The Sultan of Zanzibar has it. It was a gift to him by Mr. Cheney, but it doesn't matter. Because of it, we are free."

"Does it have any special markings on it?"

"Yes," answered Duma, wondering why this strange young man was pursuing this topic so aggressively. "It has my mark, the mark of the cheetah.

Jason responded, "Don't you mean a cat's paw print under the head of the serpent on the left, and each of the two serpents has two red beads for eyes?"

Jason's words caused a moment of immediate silence.

"How do you know that, Jason?" asked a shocked Duma.

"Because, Duma, I have your cane."

Astounded, Duma was flushed with excitement. But, why was this young black man trying to torture him so?

"Surely you just made a lucky guess Jason. You could not possibly have my cane. It is in Zanzibar."

"I have seen it many times, years ago. I used to play with it in my father's library when I was a child," said Jason, now even more certain that he was right.

"It can't be…" said Duma. "Describe it more, please."

It became an undeniable fact as Jason continued, "It appeared to have been constructed out of small pieces and cleverly assembled somehow. I remember how I used to hold it up to my father's bright reading light. I could see how the joints were made, like a…a…."

"A bird's wing bones?" Duma asked softly almost fearing the answer.

"That's it, sockets, little sockets holding the pieces together, and there was one other thing. There was a clearly carved mark under the head of the other serpent on the right side of the cane."

"What kind of a mark?"

"A letter 'V,' upside-down like a roof top."

"Or a mountain," said Duma, completely exhausted. "That is the secret mark of my brother, Mlima. He must have put it there."

"Duma, if the man who made that mountain mark on the cane, is your brother, Mlima, then we are of the same blood, for after you last saw him, he became known as el Baba, my father's grandfather.

"How could this be?" Duma asked, slumping down on the table.

CHAPTER SEVENTEEN
To break a trust

DUMA HARDLY NOTICED the ride back to his room at the Cheney House that night. He was confused beyond reality with too many unanswered questions swirling through his mind. *"How can this Jason be the great grandson of my brother, there hasn't been enough time? Yet, I'm certain of something? He has seen my serpent cane and knew Mlima's mountain mark. Is this some kind of magic, or a real miracle?"*

By the time he arrived home, he had decided that he'd have to go back to the Winters' place and find out more. *"There has to be an answer, and it is locked up, somehow, inside this Jason."*

The wagon ride into work the next morning with Billy and the new hires had only one topic, it was the revelation that somehow, Jason and Duma were strangely related. The kids knew that they would have to tell about what they knew, but they couldn't tell anyone how they knew it. The rules were clear. They weren't allowed to tell anyone about the Gothart Collection's effects other than members. It seems that what they had discovered the night before was nothing but a big problem for everyone.

Billy hadn't slept well last night either, and as he held the reins of the mules, he couldn't help his mind from going over again and again all the details of the night before.

"Lived on this earth quite a while now and I sees lots of strange things," he thought, *"but I ain't never hear'd anything likes I hear'd last night. Sumpin's not right with those three in the back of this old cart and I intend to find out."*

It was still plenty early in the morning when they got to the ivory shop. It was going to be a hot day, as summer days often are in New England. Yankee reliability and industriousness was evident already; the workers began to arrive with the expected bustle that mornings create. Jason had stayed with Billy up at the livery, and Jonah waited inside the Pratt Read factory for someone to give him an assignment while Samantha, her mind just full of worry about Jason and Duma, walked down the road and into the field to enter Bleach House Number One. It reminded her of a greenhouse, the kind you'd see often on a ride in the New Hampshire countryside, north of Boston, where people traveling would stop to buy their garden seeds and plants, and sometimes, even hanging baskets of flowers.

Sam Waterfield and a few other workers were already hard at work. He was leaning over a cart full of small pencil length rectangles of ivory veneer and placing them onto flat wooden tables. The entire bleach house was filled mostly with those same ivory veneers, all leaning and looking up at the morning sun.

"Good morning, Miss Samantha," he said cheerfully. "Can you hear the music yet?" he asked.

"Music?"

"Don't you hear it?" he joked.

"Do you mean those birds singing, Mr. Waterfield?"

"No, the piano music. That's what we make here, beautiful music on these piano keys." He held his hands up and moved his fingers as if he were actually playing a piano.

"At least he's not as grumpy as that man who hired us yesterday," Sam thought to herself, *"Poor Jonah has to work with him.*

"What do I do for work?" she asked.

"You'll be working with Amanda Johnson over there. She'll show you what we do out here. Did you bring a lunch?"

"Billy Winters says he'll drop off our lunches at noontime."

Down the long row of ivory, a lady was bending over, and moving ivory into crates in neat stacks. When she stood up and turned around, Samantha wasn't quite ready for the surprise. It was, Miss Margaret, the librarian.

"Miss Margaret!" Sam exclaimed.

"Well hello Miss…I'm Amanda Johnson. You must be the new girl?"

Catching herself, Sam corrected her words. "Oh, I'm sorry, you look like my old school mistress, Miss Amanda," and then dropping her voice to a whisper said, "Wow, am I ever glad to see you here too, Miss Margaret. Did the professor come with you this time?"

"He's up the road a ways Sam. It sounds as if you might have some sort of a problem. Just wait until Waterfield leaves to get another cartful of ivory, and then we can talk freely Sam."

"Here's what we do young lady," Miss Margaret said, speaking out loud for the benefit of Sam Waterfield, who was engaged as usual with whistling a tune. "We look carefully at each piece of ivory in this section and match them up with this sample. If they're bleached white, we stack them in these crates to make room for the sun to bleach the new ones."

As soon as Sam Waterfield had pushed his ivory cart out the end of the bleach house, Sam began telling Miss Margaret about what had occurred last night at the Winters' house.

"They can figure out that something's wrong, that Jason's telling some truth, but they can't understand that he's from the future. Do you have any ideas how we can solve this problem? The Bronze Key Society's rules are that we can't tell anyone that the Gothart Collection actually moves people back in time."

"This is a serious problem Sam, but nothing that the professor can't figure out, He's always been a wonderful help on things like this."

"There's one other thing, Miss Margaret."

"Yes, Sam?"

"This coming Sunday is the day it all happens."

"What happens Sunday, Sam?"

"What we all came here to prevent, Miss Margaret, the Pratt Read Co. factory; the one that we're all working for, is going to burn down, and fifteen tons of precious ivory will be destroyed."

"Oh dear, I almost forgot? Whatever are you going to do about it Sam?"

"I have no idea, but I do know Jonah, and he's not going to let all that valuable ivory go to waste....not after all those slaves died to get it here."

"Well you can't very well move it; there's no place to hide it and...," her voice trailed off.

"Here comes Waterman again. I'll get word to the professor. He's taken the role of a priest in Chester this trip. Where are you kids staying?"

"We're boarding with the Winters, out in Billy's big white house near the edge of town."

"Hey ladies," shouted Mr. Waterman, "I just heard that we just got an order for one hundred more keyboards from Chickering Pianos. Business sure is booming these days. I'll bet we get a five cent raise this month, too."

"Great news, Sam, I could use the extra money for new seeds. My last batch got all wet and rotted," said Miss Amada winking at Samantha.

Billy, intending to, "find sum answer to all this foolishness," had invited Duma back out for dinner, making Sam a bit concerned when, after work, Duma joined them in the wagon for the ride back home.

There was hardly any laughter this time on the bumpy ride over to Billy's. Everyone's mind was too busy with confusion.

"This is mah special dish folks, so eat up and don be shy none, there's plenty of it to go round," proclaimed Billy's wife, Lucretia.

Billy Winters joined in the appreciation for his wife's fine cooking. "The Lord gives us plenty from His bounty, but He sure worked extra hard helping Lucretia put this fine pork and beans together for us folks. Help yourselves t'all you want. Ben and Freda, you go after our guests fills up first."

Not much was spoken about what was on everyone's minds until after the meal when Billy reached up for his evening cigar and invited everyone to gather at the large kitchen table, which Lucretia had just cleared.

"We had the Lord's dinner, and now it's time to talk about the Lord's truth. How'd you really know about that cane Jason?"

"My father told me the story many times of how his grandfather's brother had made it."

"But, I made that cane, Jason, only about twenty years ago," said Duma, whose biggest frustration was that he was also quite certain in his heart that this Jason was telling the truth, somehow, but how?

"What did your Daddy tell you his granddaddy's name was?" asked Billy, trying hard, to make sense of all this.

"El Baba, it was el Baba, I'm certain because I used to pretend that I was him walking with that cane when he met the queen," said Jason, thinking that he shouldn't have mentioned the queen. They never would believe him now, but he continued telling the story as every eye in the room was glued to him looking for signs of untruth.

"My father was a French Ambassador and we were always around important people. His father told him the same story that I'm telling you now. This ex-slave, el Baba, my father's grandfather, was a diplomat for the queen."

"But, I saw him taken away from the slave market in Zanzibar by the Sultan of Zanzibar's horsemen," said Duma emphatically;

he felt Billy's hand on his arm, trying to keep him calm.

"My father said that his grandfather was freed by a British officer in Zanzibar and brought to England where he met Queen Victoria, who sent him around the Empire, as her ambassador, trying to get the slave trade stopped."

"Are you really saying Jason that my brother, Mlima, that same underfed slave I last saw chained in the slave market in Zanzibar, not only knew the Queen of England, but became her own personal ambassador?"

"That's what my father told me and I heard my grandfather tell the same story when I was little. We're a proud family Duma, and we don't tell lies or make things up to sound good."

"Jason's father was an ambassador, Duma, in Paris. He's telling you the truth about that," said Samantha.

"Then he'll have to tell me how all this happened within just twenty years?" said Duma, "because it just doesn't add up, does it?"

"I can't tell you Duma, but it's all true, I swear."

"The Lord's truth Jason?" asked Billy, with a steel-eyed gaze that would make the devil himself honest.

"The Lord's truth," answered Jason, looking Billy straight in the eyes.

Letting his frustration get the better part of him, Billy jumped up, not knowing what to do, he banged his fist on the table, and he shouted, "Why should we believe you about this, Jason?"

It was just at that moment that there was a knock on the door, a kind of insistent urgent knock. It was the strangest of strangers, Father Mallory, from the Catholic Church just up the roadway in Chester.

Jonah, Sam, and Jason all looked at the man they knew as the professor, here now, back in time with them, but wearing a priest's collar.

"Well," said Billy Winters, with wry amazement, "we sure is gettin a lot of strange new visitors here lately. Come in, Reverend,

I'll bet you smelled the Lord's cookin all the way from your church in Chester."

Father Mallory stepped into the room; he was followed by an assortment of moths and light creatures that were attracted by the light in the house.

"I understand from a friend that you folks are having a bit of a problem believing, and since that's my specialty, I thought I'd offer to try to clear things up."

"That sure would be nice, real nice," said Billy, sliding a chair over for the "Reverend," to join in the conversation. "Would you like a cigar?"

It was a long lesson, but one that really didn't offer those poor confused people of Deep River even a little proof. It did establish one thing, though; we often accept things we don't understand, simply because we place our trust in other people.

"Sometimes, there are no clear answers?" Father Mallory suggested.

"Do you expect us to believe what Jason is telling us, Reverend," asked Billy, "when it don't make no sense?"

"No. I just hope you would trust him. Haven't you all had to trust someone before, when it meant a whole lot?" asked the priest.

Duma, thought about trusting the Cheneys' setting him free and taking him back here to America to do what he loved most, carve ivory.

Billy, remembered those days when he was living within the Underground Railroad, hiding in someone's walls while the slave catchers were knocking at the door. He had trusted them that hid him, black and white folks alike.

Father Mallory had said the right thing to these men and they both knew that deep inside their hearts that Jason was telling the truth. Exactly how, they would wonder the rest of their lives.

Jason rose and clasped his arms around Duma and Duma stood there with the tearful joy, knowing that this man had somehow brought closure to the one lasting pain in his life, not knowing what happened to his brother, Mlima, or el Baba, or whatever they called him after he last saw him years ago in the slave market in Zanzibar.

"There is one more little difficulty," said the priest as he pushed back his chair.

"What's that?" asked Billy, totally unprepared for the answer.

"We've got to take all of the ivory out of the Pratt Read factory Saturday night and hide it."

Billy immediately knew for certain, *"These folks is crazy. At least working with the mules there is some sense to life."*

Some moments later, after regaining his senses, he quietly asked, "He's gone now, but why would I steal from the one man who gave me my freedom, George Read?"

"Because there's going to be a big fire, and it's all going to burn up if we don't take it out of there," said the priest.

"Why would we risk losing everything that we worked so hard for all these years, jus because you say it's gonna burn?" Billy argued.

"Lots of black people died to get that ivory here. Should their lives be wasted?" said the priest, hoping to miraculously sway this honest man.

"They's already dead. Stealing a good man's ivory ain't gonna help them none."

"Saving it from destruction, Mr. Winters, isn't exactly stealing it."

Duma was torn with emotion and pleaded, "None of this makes any sense, so give us one good reason why we should help you?"

"Trust," said the priest. "I can offer you no reason, but I ask for your trust."

"How you know that factory's gonna burn down? You gonna do it?"

"Me? I can't do that. I work for the Lord," said the priest, "but I do know some things to be true that you don't, and I can't explain how.

"There's gonna be no lynching that I bring on myself," said Billy Winters.

"We'll just have to get it out of there ourselves," said Jason resolutely.

"How are you going to do that? Where are you going to hide it?" asked Duma.

"In the Lord's Church somewhere," said the priest, putting his cap on and rising to leave.

"How do you intend to get it there?" asked Duma.

"The same way it got out of Africa," said Jason. "We'll carry it on our shoulders, if we have to. Maybe we'll even find a red-eyed serpent on the way."

The next few days would be like torture for everyone involved. Some decisions have to be made with the heart, some with the head, and some with both. The last kinds are the most difficult to make.

CHAPTER EIGHTEEN
An ivory caravan in Connecticut

JONAH REMEMBERED GETTING in trouble on a reading adventure before, but he never remembered doing such a "guaranteed to lose" thing as he was about to do. But, he was certain it was doing the right thing. He believed there was no wrong in this, except letting all that ivory go to waste after so many died because of it.

As he looked at the rows of tusks stacked like cordwood in the back of the Pratt shop, he thought, *"I'll bet someone just like Duma carried all this stuff out of Tanganyika."* He slipped the extra padlock key from its rightful place onto the bench where he could reach it through the little broken window pane.

"Tomorrow night is the night. I just hope we can carry a few of those smaller tusks up to the church before Sunday morning. It's well over a mile up there."

He glanced up as the last of the workers was leaving. Over in the corner, Duma was gathering his special tools in a bag. *"Was he afraid they would burn up in the fire? If he believes that, then he ought to...."* His thoughts were interrupted by Silas Hubbard's voice.

"Are you going to stay all weekend Son? You must really like this ivory business."

"No sir, I mean, yes sir," he stammered.

"What do you mean son?"

"I like the work, but I ain't staying, Sir."

"Then get along with you now, I've got to lock up and get up to the Colt factory tonight and I haven't time for slowpokes."

"Yes Sir."

"I wonder if he saw me hide the key," Jonah asked himself as he began the short trek over to the livery.

Saturday night came slowly, the way time always does when you want to get something distasteful over with. The sun, dragging itself painfully toward the west, was still too high in the Connecticut sky at dinner time.

Not much discussion took place at the Winters' dinner table that evening. There comes a point in all disagreeable things when the talking is over and nothing else can be said. It wasn't until after Billy finished his cigar that he spoke.

"You kids need a ride back down to the factory?" he asked.

"Thanks, but not tonight, Billy. Father Mallory has a small horse and wagon," said Jason.

"You gonna do this ain't cha?"

"We have to," said Jason

"You know it's wrong Jason."

"You have to do what is right, even when it seems wrong to others, Billy," said Jason.

"It's agin the law Jason."

"So was hiding runaway slaves, Mr. Winters."

"I know. If you're foolish enough to do such a thing, you gonna need wagons Son. Take the one out in front."

"I don't know how to drive a mule Sir."

"Then I guess, I'll jus have to come along and show you."

When Jason stepped out, he was greeted with one of the strangest scenes he had ever witnessed in his life. There, sitting in Billy's wagon, waiting to go, were Jonah, Sam, and Professor Kincaid, dressed as the priest. Behind them, several other wagons full of people were all waiting for Billy to step out of the house. All Billy's kinfolk were going to help too. They were all going to trust together, or, as Billy said, with a headshake, "go to jail together, jus like thieves."

The night was dark; a noisy wind blew off of Long Island Sound. Fortunately, a good night for thieves, when there was much less chance of being seen or heard.

The little caravan of mule-driven wagons, most of which were once used to carry the ivory from the ships up the street to the factory, came to a halt in a dark field near town.

"We's gotta leave the wagons here," whispered Billy. "They's hear one wheel squeak and we's caught. We'll carry that ivory from the factory over to this field and then load it up for the ride up to that St. Joseph's Church."

Jonah, a dark figure dressed in black, careful not to knock over anything lying around, crept around the back of the factory. He found the broken pane of glass, pushed up his jacket sleeve and felt inside for the key he had hidden.

Moments later, the front doors, the big ones that open for the ivory wagons and keyboards, were pushed open; they made much too much noise.

"Put some oil on those hinges," someone whispered, "before the whole town wakes up."

"Back here," urged Jonah, pointing out a moderately sized tusk that in the daylight would display the label, "Zanzibar prime," on its base.

Jason had reached for the heavy end and Jonah started to lift his end when suddenly a hand came out of the darkest shadows and grabbed his arm.

"I'll carry this out with my kinfolk, Jonah. I've done this before, so I know how to do it." It was Duma. He would risk everything, after all.

Even Samantha and Miss Margaret carried the small tusks. Together they formed a silent procession of bodies, slipping back and forth through the dark night up to the field to deposit the heavy ivory. It was dangerous and it was hard work; it went on hour after hour well into the night.

Just for a moment, Duma thought that this was a fitting answer to those slave caravans that carried the ivory out of Tanganyika. Only this time it is different because these folks are doing it of their own free will.

Near midnight, after locking up the factory, now empty of ivory tusks, they began to ready the wagons to move out. There would be all out trouble come Monday morning if there was no fire on Sunday.

Once, toward the end, someone dropped a tusk which made a considerable noise as it bounced off the top of a wagon wheel and fell into the dew covered field. A moment later, a light went on in a nearby window, and an old man appeared holding a shotgun while a woman by his side held a candle. They both peered out for what seemed forever. Each and every one of the ivory thieves held their breath. Finally, the light went out and a few moments later the caravan began quietly moving off toward the north and Chester.

It certainly was a strange sight to see the caravan when it finally reached the church and pulled around the back in the cemetery, out of view of the road in front.

"Where we gonna put these elephant teeth, Reverend?" Billy asked.

"I hadn't really thought of it that much, Mr. Winters. To be honest with you, I didn't really expect to get this much ivory free."

"Well you better figure it out soon. That old sun will be lookin down here in the mornin and you gots lots of people comin out to see you cause it's the Lord's day."

Duma was the one who really came up with the clever idea,

though, he didn't intend to.

"If we don't hide it all tonight we may as well be in the ground with all these dead folks because that's where we're going to be come Monday."

"That's it, Duma," said Father Mallory. "We'll bury it."

"Huh," said Billy, "Do what?"

"We'll bury it right up next to the church. Somebody get some candles and grab some shovels out of that cemetery building over there, and let's get digging."

The clatter of shovels and the groans from laboring bodies, lifting the ivory and pushing it into the seemingly bottomless hole, lasted for hours. When they had finished, Duma and Jason stood together looking at the freshly dug soil in the flickering light of the candles. Duma then recalled the flickering light of the fire on the ivory caravan that evening when he saw his snake. Reaching up to his neck, he took off the ivory coin pendant he had carved with his and el Baba's marks on it and quietly pressed it into Father Mallory's hand.

"Would you put this under the grave marker, after I leave, Father?"

When the last wagon departed back to Deep River, there was one new gravesite dug up next to the Church's side entrance, and it already had an old flat grave marker, so worn that it couldn't be read.

It was a bit of luck that no one noticed the fresh grave behind the church, except for the old feeble caretaker, Silas Morgan, who wondered how he missed hearing about the funeral. He shrugged, and placed a pot of Mrs. Morgan's petunias next to the old grave marker.

CHAPTER NINETEEN
July's even hotter when there's a fire

T HE MORNING SUN kissed the very tip of the church steeples first. As in all the little towns, nestled in the hills near the mouth of the Connecticut River, people dressed in their finest clothing emerged from their homes and began making their way to services to pay homage to their Creator.

Several went directly down Main Street into Deep River passing the familiar wooden Pratt Read and Co. building where many of them worked. Nothing seemed out of place. The steamboat to New York City was again belching smoke on its way down-river. The gulls from Long Island Sound, accompanied by their usual complaining gull noises, were making their usual morning flight up-river. Busy greeting churchgoers in front of the small New England Churches were the same local ministers that met them every Sunday morning. It might be a long service today because the heat from the hazy July sun was already building up.

As curious as the entire gang of ivory thieves was about the fire that was supposed to start, none of them dared to be within miles of it, lest they be accused of starting it. Most of them wouldn't even look in the direction of the Pratt Read factory, for fear they'd be blamed if a fire really started.

Over at the Congregational Church, the preacher was just about winding up his long sermon on stealing, several parishioners were starting to beat their breasts in genuine sorrow for what they had done last night, when a young boy stood up, looked out the window and yelled, "Fire. There's a fire right here in Deep River! I can see the smoke from here."

Within seconds, men and women sprang into action, bolted out the door, and either ran or rode their wagons toward the center of town. Folks were coming from every direction to help stop the fire.

"Oh dear Lord! It's the ivory plant. I can see the flames in the air," said one rather plump woman bouncing on the passenger seat of her wagon, holding on tightly to her bonnet and the iron wagon rail at the same time.

"There's water behind the dam. Get some buckets!"

Within a few minutes there was a bucket brigade of people in their best clothes trying to toss water on the leaping flames. Chemicals inside the building were overheating rapidly, there was a loud pop, and a window blew out.

"Don't get too close. The wind is whipping around now, and it can blow those flames right back on us," shouted, Silas Carpenter, a blacksmith from down at the shipyard. Then, a few seconds later when another window exploded, he shouted, "We better back off. It's just too dangerous."

No sooner had he said that when the entire front side corner of the building and a large portion of the roof came crashing down in a shower of sparks and flying debris.

At that moment, down the road came Billy Winters in his Sunday finest clothes driving his best mule as fast as he dared. He had seen the thick black smoke from way up the North end of town and had thrown some shovels in his wagon in case they needed to shovel some dirt on the fire, but he was too late.

The reality was that everyone was too late. The fire had a

good head start while everyone was in church. The usual eyes that might have detected the blaze early were all busy gazing at Bibles and songbooks. It was several hours later when the last of the flames died down, and the ashes were doused with water. Nothing identifiable was left except the company's steel safe. All the ivory that was not moved, was gone, disintegrated. It was a sad scene and not a totally uncommon one with those old wooden factories in New England. Wood was plentiful here, but, unfortunately, it does burn easily.

No one had gone home. It was a question of who would have employment after this tragedy now. Much of the town, one way or the other, worked for Pratt and Read. Fortunately, thanks to the men who climbed the roofs and wet them down, the bleach houses were still standing, and no other buildings were lost. Most of the heads in the crowd were hanging low, and one could hear silent sobbing. This was a day that would live forever in the minds of the people of Deep River.

Billy Winters had little to say that night at dinner. The three new workers, his boarders, were packing their few things. Without a factory to work in any longer, they had declared that it was time for them to move on.

Billy, done with all his thinking, simply said, "Well I guess the good Lord done saved all that ivory jus in time folks," and then he repeated it, "jus in time."

The three kids took their bags and walked the couple of miles to Deep River to say goodbye to Duma. Knowing he wouldn't get an answer, he asked Jason one last time, "How did you know all this would happen, Jason?"

Jason just smiled and said, "You'll like the new brick factory Duma. I'll come back to see you again, someday." They embraced and parted.

Jason was grinning nervously this time as they all said the three words of the oath: "*Gothart, Trahtog, Gothart,*" moving them once again through time. It was a joyous occasion as the adventurers returned to the Gothart Room in the old McClelland Library. Actually living in the reading had proven to be an invaluable, if not an emotional, experience. This time, the newest member, Jason, had learned something personal, almost beyond all understanding. He and his father were related to a humble slave from old Tanganyika who had become a master ivory carver in southern Connecticut.

"Jason," said the professor, "this adventure certainly changes your life now, doesn't it?"

"I can't wait to tell my father what I have just learned. To think that the same ivory cane I played with all those years ago was carved by Duma."

"I know this is a silly question," said Samantha, "but what about the ivory. Is it still there in the grave that we helped to dig?"

"It should be fine," said the professor, "but we may find some problem getting any value for it. I believe the selling of ivory has been either stopped or severely restricted, due to the danger to the elephant populations."

"I've got to go to Paris to see my Dad, and to tell him about Duma and el Baba being brothers and about the cane. Dad knows a lot of people, because he was the ambassador. If we need to do something with the ivory, why don't we let him work on the solution for getting it out and sold?"

"It's of little use in the ground," said Jonah, "I agree."

"Boy, wait until Macready finds out how much we've learned about the ivory trade," said Sam.

"Macready!" We've been gone for days!" said Jason in a panicked realization.

They all laughed at his worry and informed him that no time had actually passed since they first went through the book and back in time to Deep River.

"It's still Saturday morning here in Boston," said Sam. "You'll get used to it, Jason."

"I'm not certain that anyone can get used to traveling back in time like that. It sure does seem like a dream."

"There's one thing we know though, kids," said Miss Margaret. "We know how it feels to carry elephant tusks."

"Yeah," said Jason, "Maybe Duma didn't mind as much this time."

CHAPTER TWENTY
You won't believe this Dad, but...

C HILLS RAN DOWN Jason's back as he pressed the doorbell on the old Parisian building. He was already worrying, *"How am I going to explain how I know what I know? How will I tell my dad that I had just met his great-grandfather's brother who lived in Connecticut over a hundred years ago?"* He would certainly think his son crazed to say such a thing. He almost wished now that he hadn't agreed to follow the rules of not sharing the secret to the Gothart collection with anyone. Still, he had to tell him the truth without divulging anything protected by his oath. His father not only needed to know that Duma was his relative, but he needed to know about the ivory. *"Who else will be able to figure out a way to get all that ivory out and put to good use, but Dad?"*

The old door creaked open just a bit and Jason could see an eye peering out at him. It was his older sister, Vicky; she had been Dad's eyes during his reading research these last few years.

"Dad, it's Jason. He's here in Paris!" she shouted to someone upstairs.

Rising from his table surrounded by an array of old and

valuable books, Jason's father, smiling broadly, opened his arms to his son.

"Well, this is certainly a surprise Jason, a welcome surprise, but nonetheless a surprise. What brings you to Paris during the school year?"

"I've got a week's vacation Dad, and I decided to use some of my savings to fly home."

"Don't tell me you're homesick. You've been off to other schools, longer than this?"

"We'll talk later Dad, I'm kind of worn out from the plane ride," he said. Jason wanted to avoid bringing up anything that was on his mind when his sister Victoria was around. She had that subtle, sibling way of demeaning him whenever she failed to understand much of what he said. What he had to say now to his father, she would simply never understand.

It wasn't until later that evening, after Vicky had retired, that he dared to approach his father with his real reason for coming to Paris.

"Say, Dad, I was just curious. In all your studies of ancient manuscripts and writings have you ever heard of something called the Gothart Collection?"

Trevor LeBlanc, took off his glasses, and looked in the direction of Jason. "Did you come to Paris, to inquire about a legendary set of manuscripts?"

"Well, no Sir, but I would be interested in hearing what that legend is."

"How did you hear about it, Jason?"

"A few friends mentioned it, Sir, but they know very little about the legend," he fibbed.

Cleaning his dark glasses as he often did when he was in deep thought; Trevor LeBlanc told of a story about a medieval monk who stumbled across some manuscripts that had special powers, including the ability to move through history within its pages. It seems that the ability to transfer oneself back through time was what made the legend so popular among the ancient scholars, most of whom, dismissed it as what it was, merely a legend, that's all."

Jason wasn't certain that his father was telling him all that he knew about the Gothart Collection, but he knew from experience that he would hear no more on the subject.

"So it's just a legend we can forget, after all?" Jason asked, trying to be casual about the subject.

"It depends upon your wisdom or your gullibility, I suppose," said his father, and then changing topics completely, he asked quite seriously, "Why *did* you come to Paris, Jason?"

"Well Dad, this is one of those stories that begins with: 'You're not going to believe this, but,'" he halted and immediately asked, "Do you still have that ivory cane with the two snakes on it, the one that came from that famous grandfather of yours from Zanzibar?"

"Why yes, Jason. El Baba's cane is by the door downstairs in the umbrella rack. I use it, now and then, when I go for a walk."

"What would you say if I told you, Dad, that I met the man who carved it over a hundred years ago?"

Once again Trevor LeBlanc took out a wrinkled handkerchief from his pocket and began deliberately rubbing the already cleaned lens of his glasses. After a period of time in deep thought, he said, "Go on, Jason."

"Well, I can't tell you how because I made a promise to someone, but this is what happened to me. I think I can prove what I say, Dad, but you'll have to go to America to find that out."

"Continue with what you have to say Jason," his dad said, suppressing the urge to clean his glasses again.

It was a couple of hours later when Jason concluded his tale. Reaching the precarious part, his father's reaction, he concluded anxiously.

"I've often wondered about those two odd marks on that cane,

Jason. I just dismissed it as some sort of religious symbolism from Africa," said his Father. "If this is a true story Jason, and if there is a grave full of ivory near a church in Connecticut; what would you have me do about it?"

"Dad, what would our enslaved relatives, Duma and el Baba, want you to do about it?"

Once again, Trevor's glasses received a thorough cleaning, and then, he paused once more before he made the decision Jason was looking for.

"I'll call the airline in the morning and order two tickets: one for, you, Son, to return to school in Boston, and another for me to rendezvous with whoever is now the priest in Connecticut, that is after I do a little research on the matter at hand."

They both stood and embraced once more. Jason knew he had made the right judgment; he could rely on his father to believe him.

As they both moved off to retire for the night, Trevor LeBlanc had one last question.

"This Duma fellow Jason, is he as handsome as you?"

CHAPTER TWENTY-ONE
There are tons of ivory down there

LEANING FORWARD AND resting his stubble-bearded chin on his ivory cane, the man in the damp dark suit took off his dark glasses, pulled a wrinkled handkerchief from his coat pocket and began ritually cleaning the lenses as he finished telling this Connecticut priest the last of his enchanting story.

"...and so you see Father Novak, I'm the man that was once a French ambassador, and relative of both those brothers, the slaves from old Tanganyika. Jason is my son. This is an impossible story I know, but in that old grave out there, there are tons of ivory tusks."

Father Novak was in deep thought as he busied himself with cleaning the mess from his spilled coffee.

"Mrs. Cornish's hand-crocheted doily," he said, holding it up in a detached manner. "I hope I haven't ruined it."

"You don't believe me, of course, Father," said Trevor LeBlanc.

"But you offer no proof as to how it got there."

The priest, having just listened to the most far-fetched tale of his life, was trying hard to synthesize his contradictory feelings.

That this man was being honest, he was certain. That his story was true, was far less certain.

"I have heard of many a strange thing in my life as a priest, but this is the first time anyone has claimed to know secrets about the past with such certainty. You realize that all we have to do in order to verify your, ah, story, is to dig up that area?"

"You'll need to do it carefully Father; ivory, especially prime Zanzibar ivory, is quite valuable these days."

"So what would you have us do with the ivory that you say is in that grave should we ever decide to dig it up?"

"Look Father, I can understand your not believing me because I found it more than difficult to believe my own son when he told me the same story."

"So what caused you finally to believe him then?" asked the priest.

"Well for one thing, he didn't fly all the way to Paris to tell me a lie. For another, I have never known him to be deceitful before and the last, but the most important reason. It is the same reason that your predecessor, Father Mallory believed; we all have, sometimes in life, to live not only by what we can prove but by what we believe. We simply just have to trust. Isn't that what you do, Father, trust?"

"I prefer to call if faith, Mr...."

"At last, perhaps this man will now tell me his name."

"LeBlanc, Trevor LeBlanc."

"You're of course named after...?"

"Trevor Southerland, Captain, Trevor Southerland. He was my late grandfather, el Baba's, best friend and companion."

"And your daughter, Victoria, you have named her after this el Baba's favorite queen, no doubt?"

"Yes, fascinating story isn't it?"

"Yes."

"You never answered my question though. What would, what should I do if I were to, shall I say, miraculously, find that grave to be full of expensive ivory?"

"You're a man of justice. How would you use such sudden wealth to rectify, even a little, the loss of millions of African lives, caused by man's attraction to ivory?"

"You'd leave the decision up to me, then?"

"Yes."

"Isn't it now prohibited to sell ivory?"

"I believe under present international ivory law it is, but there is an exception made for selling old ivory, and this particular ivory certainly qualifies for that."

"I'm still not certain that I care to make the decision to dig. The grave is in sacred ground after all."

"What if I offered some real proof to you that it isn't a real grave?"

"What proof could you offer, short of digging it all up, Mr. LeBlanc?"

"Do you have a tire iron around?"

"Yes, in the car."

"Then put on your coat and get it. I'll meet you at the grave marker."

"Won't you need some assistance getting out to the marker?"

"I can still see well enough. It's just mostly in reading my books that I need a bit of help to see," said the man with confidence, "but I'll need your help lifting that old grave marker from its place."

The freezing rain had subsided now, though it was still bitter cold and damp; the two men made their way over to the church.

"You really believe that we're standing above tons of ivory and not the well corrupted bones of some past parishioner, don't you, Mr. LeBlanc?"

"We'll each know the answer to that in a few minutes, Father." Both men jabbed and tugged at the old mildewed marker trying to wedge it loose from its long time home in the frozen soil. Finally, it gave way, and slid out over onto the icy turf nearby.

One of the men reached down and pried something up from the frozen earth. It was a stained ivory pendant containing the still visible images of a cheetah's paw print on the left side and what could easily be a symbol of a mountain on the right.

A half dozen feet under the frozen earth, tons of ivory tusks, once carried on the back of slaves and brought here years ago from Zanzibar, were about to be resurrected.

CHAPTER TWENTY-TWO
But, who is to blame?

"OKAY CLASS, LET'S settle down now. Today's the last day we have on this Post-Emancipation Slavery unit before the big test, and I think we need to bring some of what we found in our research to the attention of the others. I know you're all eager to participate."

A loud groan came from the back of the class. It was Marsha Whitely.

"What's the problem, Marsha, didn't you do your research?"

"No, it's not that, Mr. Macready. I forgot my folder on the spice trade and I had some neat stuff in there, but I did bring these," she said proudly holding up a box of little jars full of spices.

"Oh, that's very clever of you young lady. Now would you care to pass them around so that we can all be reminded of just one of the things slavery gave to the world?"

"Mr. Macready, I found out that the lives of the slaves, who worked the spice fields and were later set free by the British, did not change all that much," said Marsha. "Now, they still have to work the same spice plantations and they barely survive."

"That's true Marsha; they hardly make but a few pennies a day even now, but what is the issue we're dealing with, poverty or slavery?"

"Some people would argue there's not much difference," said George.

"Some people would argue anything George, but isn't it possible that rich people could be slaves also?"

"Huh?" said George, surprised by the question.

"Well let's take the proverbial wealthy man who can't exist without making money or counting it every day, George, the kind of person who jumps off of buildings when the stock market collapses. Wouldn't we have to also call an uncontrolled attachment to money a type of slavery if we're going to accept just the amount of wealth one has as the criteria for enslavement?"

"I suppose…."

"What about drugs or food, then?" asked Samantha. "Lots of people are slaves to different things."

"Good, Sam, except in this unit we will be talking about physical slavery only, so we'll limit it to that, unless you have a good reason class."

"Shouldn't we add one more word to our definition before we go too far?" asked Will Connors.

"And what word is that, Will?"

"'Forced. Lots of people have submitted themselves to slavery voluntarily."

"Such as?"

"Such as, when our country was just starting, many people willingly signed onto slavery and promised to work for someone as their servant if they paid for their passage over here. It's indentured slavery, or something like that."

"That's true and an excellent point. So we'll also leave out voluntary servitude right now. Once more, class, today we're only talking about involuntary forced physical slavery. Got it?"

It was right then that Jonah started sneezing. After a dozen or so very loud interruptions, it was agreed that Marsha Whitely's spices would be put back in their box, at least the peppers.

"I was surprised to learn that Native Americans were used as slaves in Europe for awhile, Mr. Macready," said George, "until they were later replaced by Africans."

"Yes but, post-emancipation slavery George. We're only dealing with what occurred after our Civil War. That was much earlier in history."

"Some slavery is still going on in parts of Africa," said Jason, "in the Sahara region."

"That's true Jason, and an excellent point. Would you say that it is forced labor for growing or making products for the marketplace?"

"I think it's just about keeping some folks in charge of others, but it's not about world trade or anything like that, just local economics."

"I have a question to ask the class, and it'll probably show up somewhere on your exam, but we need to keep our passions under control here, so that we can really examine and learn from our discussion. Does everyone understand that?" asked Mr. Macready.

"Fire away," said Jonah. "We're ready."

"I hope so," said Macready, still not quite certain that he should ask this particular question.

"Alright, it's just a three word question and I'm going to ask that we limit our discussion to the ivory trade because that deals with us here in New England in a special way. Here it is. Who was guilty?"

"White people."

"Omani Arabs."

"Black tribal chiefs."

"Rich ivory buyers."

"Those two Connecticut companies."

"Everyone who used ivory."

"Piano players," shouted someone.

"Slow elephants," quipped Eddie, the proverbial class clown, bringing any serious discussion to a rapid halt.

"Thanks for your brilliant insight, once again, Eddie. But class, doesn't Eddie's humor raise another valid point? Is it the ivory itself that's at fault? When the demand for its beauty got so high, its economic value made the ivory caravans well worthwhile. Let me put it still another way. Was it the allure of the ivory that caused the demand for ivory products, which then caused slavery?"

"Hmmmm," said Eddie, always much smarter than he pretended to be, "You could ask the same question about drug users today and the warfare among growers, dealers and pushers."

"You could Eddie, but we won't, only because we're talking about ivory. One more time class, is the product the real cause of slavery?"

"Of course not," said Jason, remembering the discussion back in Deep River.

"If that were true, anyone who used tobacco, or wore cotton and used spices would be guilty, and that would include blaming Scott Joplin for helping to make piano playing popular. All of this stuff is just about the products that the slave labor helped bring to the marketplace. Slavery is not things. It's people that are the slaves and other people that make them slaves. I think we have two causes of slavery. Both of them called man."

"Could you explain in a little more detail, Jason? Perhaps, you could give us an example of something?"

"Well the first one would have to be man's greed, and not what he's greedy for. When there's a lot of easy money around it seems that lots of people do a lot of immoral things they ought not to do in order to get it. Much of that ivory was lying around parts of Africa for years and few people there even cared about it, until they found out people far away would pay plenty for it.

So, you see, just about everybody, in every way possible, tried to make an easy profit off of the ivory trade."

"Good point and the other thing about why man is the cause, is…?"

"Well it wasn't necessary to use black people to get that ivory out, but it was plenty efficient, Heck, black people were used for slavery for centuries, long before the ivory trade, because they came cheap, cheaper than pack mules, and that is the problem. When man thinks black people, or any people for that matter, are just like animals, no better at all, he'll begin treating them like animals. Thinking your enemy isn't worth much, causes a lot of wars also. Until we stop thinking about all humans as anything less than special like ourselves, it's going to continue. The only reason we're serious about stopping the ivory trade today is because now lots of people worry about folks killing off the elephants. No one was really too excited all those years about killing off humans for ivory, but animals are somehow important enough to make it stop. Something is upside-down here, Mr. Macready."

There were a few moments of silence in the classroom as Jason's thoughts began to sink in, and then Macready raised another point that he felt needed to be mentioned.

"Okay class. We might all disagree as to where the guilt is, but there is another element here that's also important for you to learn. How is it that this slave-based ivory trade could take place for so many years after America and Europe had both already rejected slavery altogether?"

"I'll try that," said Jonah. "Like those people in those two Connecticut towns, they all had jobs because of it."

"Maybe," said George, always the class thinker. "It's true that it was about money, indirectly, but the ivory business wasn't about having slaves produce it over here like our cotton and tobacco. It was different, because it was mostly happening elsewhere, and the product was brought over here without our ever seeing the slaves."

"Bingo George, you've nailed it," said Macready, glancing at the clock.

"I'm going to have to cut it off here because time is short, class," said Macready, "but I want you to think about this. It is often said that no one would ever eat sausage if they watched it being made. Could it be that it's easier to accept slavery, or any evil for that matter, if it's also done out of sight?"

After leaving a moment for that important message to sink in, he continued, "The last thing today is an article I found in the Times this weekend and I'd like to read it to you. I know you'll find it interesting."

"Dodoma, Tanzania:

The Tanzanian Council of Interior Affairs announced today the reception of a grant for three million dollars designated for the development of a series of monuments to be placed along the centuries-old ivory caravan routes between the country's interior and Bagamoya and Zanzibar. These monuments will be testimonials to the spirits of those who paid with their lives and freedom on the ivory trails of old Tanganyika."

"And now for the big thriller, class...."

"The money was obtained from the internationally approved sale of approximately fifteen tons of old ivory by an anonymous Connecticut church and donated to the Tanzanian government to be used solely for this purpose."

Jason turned to Jonah and Sam, and sharing the sheer joy of the moment, dared to whisper, "Where are we going to next time?"

CHAPTER TWENTY-THREE
The ivory is gone now

I T WAS ONE of those small well-worn and poorly cared for cemeteries, often found tucked in seldom trod corners of towns, the kind that you could find most anywhere in rural America. The Deep River town clerk had informed Jason and his Dad that it was just her guess as to who was buried there, and then she gave them perfect directions to the little iron-railed area behind the tall groove of stately hemlock trees.

A short distance away down by the river, the bustle of pleasure boats now fills the lower Connecticut River air and the dock area no longer holds the frames of the massive nineteenth century sailing ships that were once built there. The shad still arrive here faithfully in the spring, but few men ply the old trade of hauling nets by hand for a living anymore. There are no longer any squeaky-wheeled wagons filled with ivory and led by horses and mules, hauling loads up from the river. The old piano keyboard factory, rebuilt in 1882 to replace the Pratt Read building, no longer employs workers to process ivory. It has been converted to living quarters now. Evidence of the great ivory era is scant, limited to a marker or two in front of an Inn, a playhouse, or a cemetery plot. Street signs display the names of some of those who played a part in that earlier world; Pratt Street, Read Street and Winter Ave. A map mentions without fanfare, names like Ivory Pond, Bleach Pond and Keyboard Pond. It's true that an unkempt bleach house from earlier days still exists, but mostly for the benefit of those few history buffs who would come here for something other than a play, a fine meal, or access to the fishing and sailing nearby.

Down the road, just a healthy walk away, is Ivoryton; the town built from nearly nothing in order to provide a life for the imported immigrant workers of the Comstock Cheney ivory plant. Upriver, a couple of miles, nestled just off the road, is a Catholic church with a new addition now, where an old grave once graced the soil.

Up on a hill in Deep River, two men bend over an old gravestone, pry it loose with a tire iron, it releases. One of the men leans over and places under it a half of an old ivory pendant with the design of a cheetah paw print carved on it. They put the grave marker back in its original place, and pause, once more, to read its barely legible inscription:

"HE WHO CARVES IS FREE."

They turn away, one leans a bit on a fine ivory cane composed of two entwined serpents; the other clutches the other half of an ivory pendant, that will be placed under a grave marker somewhere in France.